OSAMA BIN LADEN'S PERSONAL DIARY

Osama Bin Laden's Personal Diary

2003–2004

iUniverse, Inc.

New York Lincoln Shanghai

Osama Bin Laden's Personal Diary
2003–2004

iUniverse books may be ordered through booksellers or by contacting:

iUniverse
2021 Pine Lake Road, Suite 100
Lincoln, NE 68512
www.iuniverse.com
1-800-Authors (1-800-288-4677)

ISBN-13: 978-0-595-38095-4 (pbk)
ISBN-13: 978-0-595-82463-2 (ebk)
ISBN-10: 0-595-38095-6 (pbk)
ISBN-10: 0-595-82463-3 (ebk)

Printed in the United States of America

Foreword

This book does not oppose the religion of Islam, nor any other venerable system of belief. It is, however, critical of bigotry, hatred, hypocrisy and any form of fundamentalism.

The author views humor, tolerance and understanding as the most effective antidotes to such fanaticism.

D.C.

Some of the names mentioned in the Diary (in order of appearance)

Osama bin Laden. Leader of al-Qaeda. Also known as The Director, The Prince and The Emir. Still at large.

Kim Jong-il, President of North Korea.

Fazul Abdullah Mohammed, from the Cormoros Islands, reputed to be al-Qaeda's IT specialist. Still at large.

Ayman al-Zawahiri, deputy head of al-Qaeda. Also known as the Doctor, the Teacher, the Egyptian, Abu Abdallah and Abu Mohammed. Still at large.

Khalid Shaikh Mohammed, who conceived of and directed the September 11 attacks. Now held by the Americans.

Abu Hamza al Jazeeri. Osama bin Laden's personal bodyguard. Algerian.

Mullah Omar. The one-eyed leader of the Taliban, which was eventually defeated in 2001. Omar, like his son-in-law, Osama bin Laden, is now on the run.

Salim Mohammed bin Laden, Osama's eldest brother. Died in a flying accident in Texas in 1988.

Pervaiz Musharraf. President of Pakistan.

Mohammed Atta. Local commander of the 9/11 hijackers and the pilot of American Airlines Flight 11 which flew into the North Tower of the World Trade Center.

Fatima. One of bin Laden's wives, and daughter of Mullah Omar, the Taliban leader.

George Tenet. The then head of the CIA.

Khan. A little known Afghanistan warlord.

Sayyid Qutb. Pakistani scholar, philosopher and father of modern fundamentalism. Hanged in Egypt in 1966.

Bin Laden's diaries (covering the years 2003-2004) were discovered in a cave near the summit of Kuh-e-Qeusar (4,182 meters), north-west of Kandahar, in Afghanistan. The cave had been evacuated in great haste following a raid by American Special Forces acting on a tip-off from a recently captured local warlord. Food was still cooking on the fire and a television set was switched on (to The Simpsons.*)*

The al-Qaeda terrorists who had been holed up in the cave only had time to grab their rifles and, in the case of bin Laden, his laptop computer. No one was captured in that raid. The diaries were not hidden; rather they appear to have been accidentally dropped during the rushed exodus from the cave. They were picked up by a Special Forces officer who, for reasons of personal safety, wishes to remain anonymous. On his return to the States, he contacted a literary agent. The diaries were translated at great speed and, just two months after their discovery, are already available to the general public.

The diaries provide a fascinating insight into the mind of the al-Qaeda leader, his motives and beliefs as well as his organizational abilities. As to their authenticity, experts are, for once, in absolute agreement: no one could forge such documents; they are simply too authentic.

Acknowledgements

When researching this book, I received invaluable insight and information from several sources, and I am especially grateful to the following authors:
Karen Armstrong's *Islam* (U.K., Weidenfeld & Nicolson, 2000), Ann Gerhart's *The Perfect Wife* (U.S., Simon & Schuster, 2004), Kitty Kelley's *The Family* (U.S., Anchor Books, 2005), Adam Robinson's *Bin Laden* (Scotland, Mainstream Publishing, 2001), Malise Ruthven's *A Fury for God* (U.K., Granta Books, 2002), and Bill Sammon's *Misunderestimated* (U.S., Regan Books, 2004). D.C.

2003

January 1.

My piles are acting up.

The US and the UK are pouring troops into the Gulf region in preparation for the invasion of Iraq. They are rushing to their own graves. No—they are like drops of water falling onto the sands of the desert.

(That is more poetic, I think.)

January 6.

It will be warm in Iraq now. It reminds me of my childhood in Saudi Arabia, always having the sun on my face. I imagine the sand, the swaying palm trees, walking along a beach by the Red Sea, outside Jiddah, and watching the tankers queuing up to go through the Canal. Here it is so cold, so windy and miserable. Just snow, snow and more snow. I hate being cold all the time, and it plays havoc with my chilblains.

I was born in a land of sand. It was a part of your life, it was everywhere: in your sandwiches, between your toes, in your eyes, in your bed and in your car. It even used to find its way between your woman's legs, for goodness sake. What abrasion! And now this sand has been replaced by snow. It freezes you to the bone, soaks you right through, numbs you and blinds you. What would I give to live in a land that was somewhere between these two extremes. There I'd be happy. One day, when I am no longer being hunted, I shall live in such a country.

January 8.

I picture George swaggering across the school playground in Midland, Texas, tall for his age, white and well fed, his socks round his ankles, picking his snotty nose with a dirty finger, a few hangers-on behind him. He goes up to some swarthy Middle Eastern kid who has wandered into the playground from some school at the rough end of town. He's standing by himself: he has shifty eyes, greasy hair and an incipient moustache.

"You the one who's been picking on my Dad?'

The foreign kid looks uneasy. "Maybe." He shrugs, trying to look indifferent.

The white kid puzzles over this answer, like it wasn't clear cut enough for him. The troops behind him are getting restless. Suddenly the foreign kid reaches into his satchel, and someone shouts out: "Watch it, George, he's got a weapon!"

"Quick, hit him," says one nerdy looking individual with glasses and a neat schoolboy haircut. "He's got a knife, and he's laughing at you." And, sure enough, there was a faint smile on the foreign boy's lips.

"Yeah, kick him in the nuts," says another friend, a fat boy with a potato head, glasses and a crew cut. "Remember what he did to your Dad. He's a stoolie, George. Go on, belt him, then you'll be number one on the campus!"

And that seems to make up George's mind for him. He hits the boy in the mouth, right on his smile, making him fall over on his backside. His hand comes out of his satchel, but he's not holding a knife or anything else.

"He ain't got a knife," says someone.

"That don't matter. He could have done."

Then, right on cue, all the white kids turn around and there, coming through the school gates, is a crowd of all the foreign boy's friends and relatives from the tough neighborhood across town…

January 12.

Not only has North Korea withdrawn from the Nuclear Nonproliferation Treaty, but the dwarf Kim Jong-il has promised that the US will disappear in "a sea of fire" if it continues to challenge his country. Mr. Platform Shoes has spunk—a man after my own heart. Must phone him and congratulate him on his fine oratory and exceptional diplomatic skills.

January 15.

Ali infuriates me. He has taken my yoghurt, and it's not the first time. He knows I love yoghurt, and yet he's stolen the very last of mine. It wasn't the communal yoghurt; it belonged to me. I won't have any now for the next few days, until supplies come up from the village. He is so inconsiderate, not to say dishonest, because I'm sure he knows it was mine. Quite honestly, he doesn't seem to give a damn.

He took his headphones off. I could hear *Terrorist* by D.J. Vadim. That's all he ever listens to. When I confronted him about the yoghurt, he barely tried to deny it. "So?" he said, and his attitude was really quite belligerent. His presence can be intimidating. He's the same height as me, around six foot three inches, but he's broader.

"So?" Like, well, you want to make something out of this? He can make himself look seriously menacing when he wants to. Actually, he doesn't even have to try. He looks seriously menacing without any effort at all on his part. He only has one eyebrow, that's what does it: just a big overhang of black hair from the outside corner of one eye to the outside corner of the other, without any kind of break in the middle. He also wears a headband. I think he sees himself as some kind of Arabian Rambo.

He doesn't give me the respect I'm due, that's for sure. Of course, I have to be careful what I say to him—we all do—because he's such a head case. Although I'm a little wary of him most of the time, I was really forceful and outspoken with him this morning. This yoghurt stealing has happened once too often.

"Ali," I said, "I was just wondering if you didn't by any chance, by mistake of course, take some of my yoghurt yesterday, did you?" This was speaking plainly, telling him exactly what's what.

But all he did was to shrug his shoulders, put his headphones back over his ears, and say, "So? I may have done. So?"

What can you do with a person like that, someone who's so thoughtless and selfish? I gave him one of my withering looks, turned my back on him as cool as anything, and with quiet dignity and head held high, strode away. That certainly showed him how I felt.

What really irked me about the whole affair was that I had put my name on the container. In big letters: OSAMA. In felt pen. A blind man couldn't have missed it. I know the man is pig ignorant, but surely even he can read a name on a tub of yoghurt. More like he just chose to ignore it.

January 16.

Just stumbled across the Paris Hilton video on some porn site. I fail to see her appeal. It was a bit like watching a skeleton in an aerobics class. Me, I like the mature woman—like Laura Bush. Full figured, maybe sagging a little here and there, but ripe. Good, child-bearing hips, and plenty of meat. I'm sure she's not getting it from George. He's in bed by nine from what I hear, and she doesn't join him until hours later. She has to be frustrated.

How can I get her to Afghanistan? If she were to see my caves, meet my followers, experience the excitement of my life and marvel at the majesty of the surrounding mountains, I'm certain she would fall for me. Maybe I should offer to negotiate with the enemy, but only on condition she was the one to come out and negotiate on their behalf?

I should also buy more books. That would impress her: she likes books from what I hear. And all I have on my shelf in one of the caves right now is some Harry Potter, Tom Clancy, Jackie Collins and Arthur Hailey. I'm sure she wouldn't have read them all, but it wouldn't do any harm to get some more in. Maybe some erotica, a few bodice rippers, to get her in the mood?

If she refused all my ministrations, I could always try Cherie Blair. She's pretty hot, too.

January 18.

Had this dream last night.

There was this open-top Hummer driving round and round between gushing oil wells, and big, black droplets of oil were falling from the sky. And the Hummer was being driven by Bush in a Stetson, with Condo sitting on top of the passenger seat, one hand resting on his shoulder, and they were grinning at each other like idiots, laughing at the oil splashing all over them. And standing outside a tent on top of a nearby sand dune was Cheney, dressed all in khaki, his little knobbly knees exposed beneath his shorts. And the three of them were singing:

Oil drops keep falling on my head

Those oil drops are falling on my head, they keep falling.

Oil drops keep falling on my head but that doesn't mean my eyes will soon be turning red.

Crying's not for me cause I'm never gonna stop the oil by complaining. Because Iraq's free. Nothing's worrying me.

January 20.

I have a wife in Kandahar, a wife in Khartoum, and a wife in Jiddah, and what good does it do me? None! My palm tree needs an oasis.

This abstinence problem has been much on my mind recently (and not just my mind), so much so I believe my frustration has become obvious to Mohammed. We have known each other since my university days in Jiddah, so he understands me better than anyone. He is the same age as me, older than the others around me (apart, that is, from the Doctor.) Even though he is lazy, he is a good man. He will do anything for me. That became obvious to me today.

His wife, Samah, is here with us. She does not move from cave to cave every time we move, because she is only a woman and would get in our way. But he sees her at least once a fortnight, and when they get back together everyone can hear their joyful reunion. She sounds a very passionate woman. She is pretty, too, although she is a good woman and hides her face behind the hijab(1) at all times. But I can tell from the eyes. To a man of passion, such as myself, the eyes of a woman will reveal the whole body. And from the way she moves he can fill in the rest.

This afternoon I was alone in the cave, apart from Ahmed, a raw recruit recently arrived from Lahore. He was on duty at the entrance. I was at my computer as usual, in the curtained off area at the back of the cave. I was sending a message to one of our sleepers in Rome, and was quite absorbed in my task, when I heard a small voice call out, "Sir, it is me, Samah."

Somewhat surprised I answered, "Hello, Samah, what do you want?"

"May I come in?" she asked. This surprised me even more. I scarcely expect to be interrupted when I am working, especially by a woman.

"Yes, of course, you may." I thought I should be polite to the wife of my old friend. She came through the curtain into my private quarters. "Can I help you?" I asked.

"Why no, sir, I am sorry if I disturbed you, it's just that I am a little bored." She seemed a little flustered. This I noticed.

"You're not disturbing me, Samah." I turned to face her. "Where is Mohammed?" I asked.

"Oh, he is out, sir. He has gone across to see Hamzah (who was in a cave complex to the east.) He is checking the lie of the land, and won't be back for some time," she added, I thought, a little unnecessarily.

Checking the lie of the land is something the men do several times a day. They leave the caves and check, often with the help of binoculars, the surrounding mountains in order to make sure there are no Americans in the area. It is an added precaution, and scarcely necessary, because Americans like to announce their presence with the subtlety of a camel in a crowded market place. Black Hawk and Apache helicopters thunder overhead, orders are shouted from one mountaintop to the next, and rifle shots frequently ring out. (Usually they are shooting at figments of their imagination.) Once the Americans arrive on the scene, it can be difficult to remain ignorant of their presence.

Samah now stood before me, looking increasingly nervous, her fingers busy with her beads. I quickly realized she was overawed being alone in my presence.

"Sit down," I said pulling up a chair, trying to put her at her ease.

"Oh no, thank you, sir, I couldn't do that."

I have to admit I had rarely paid any attention to the woman. She had always just been there, in the background, cooking, doing the dishes, sweeping the floor of the cave or washing the men's clothes. I had scarcely said two words to her in as many years. We should have had a lot to talk about, I thought, but it didn't seem that we did.

"Are you very busy," I asked politely, trying to put the young thing at ease. (I think she's a good twenty years younger than Mohammed.)

"Oh no, sir. I have already prepared our meal for this evening. I have time on my hands."

Only at that moment did the thought occur to me as to why she could be standing before me, why she had come to visit me. Could Mohammed, God protect him, have sent her, his own wife, to comfort me, to offer me solace? Had he taken pity on his friend's lamentable and enforced state of chastity?

The rate at which it was beating, my heart certainly believed it to be so. Allah be praised for such generosity of spirit—if that is what it was. I felt stirrings beneath my robes, but told myself to be careful: it would be an unfortunate mistake if I was to jump to the wrong conclusion and leap on my oldest friend's wife.

I stared at her in silence. She had her head down. She wouldn't look at me. I found myself imagining the ripe roundness beneath her robe, the roseate nipples and the young, firm flesh.

I determined to steer our conversation into a more fruitful area. I had to encourage her to reveal why she was with me if I was to prove my suspicions were correct.

"At your tender age, Samah, you will find it difficult—if not impossible—to understand what a terrible strain it can sometimes be for a person such as myself heading up such a large and important worldwide organization."

"Oh yes, it must be, sir," she said, obviously relieved to find something we could talk about.

"The stress can be quite severe."

"I am certain of that," she said. "Everyone has the greatest respect for you, sir, and what you do."

"Yes, I do know that." I smiled modestly.

She looked up at me for just a second. Her eyes were earnest, innocent and full of admiration. They had given her away. My heart pounded.

"And for a leader such as myself, out in the field 365 days of the year, worrying ceaselessly about the welfare of my followers, there is no…How can I best put this? There is no…well, *relief.* Everything builds up. In your head, in your…in your…Well, everywhere, Samah, everywhere." I wondered if she was following me.

She nodded, but kept her head down. I pictured her blushing furiously. After weeks of lying dormant, my palm tree stirred, doubtless fueled by this sudden glimmer of hope. I folded my hands across it, trying to hide it, not wanting to startle her—not yet.

"I have not seen any of my wives for a long time, Samah. That is my dilemma."

"I understand, sir."

"But do you, Samah?" I cried out for sympathy.

She looked startled. I had not wished to frighten her, but decided then and there that I must ask the question that would clarify everything.

"Does Mohammed know you are here with me now?"

For a moment, she did not move. Her fingers even froze on her beads. She did not say anything, simply nodded her head slowly. I watched, fascinated, as her fingers again started to work furiously on her beads. The tension was palpable. A minute later, she cleared her throat and said:

"Yes, sir, he knows." It was said in the quietest of voices. "He is happy for me to be with you, sir. He is your most devoted disciple. He would do anything for you."

I did not need any more encouragement. I reached out and pulled the young girl towards me. She can only have been about twenty, and I appreciated what an honor this would be for her, to have the head of al-Qaeda enter her most sacred sanctum.

She stood before me, docile, like a lamb. I lifted her robe. Her bush was black and dense, spreading across the tops of her thighs. My palm tree, already erect, became, if such a thing is possible, even more erect at the proximity of this beautiful hidden crevasse. I could barely control myself. My weeks of frustration were about to end.

I lay my head against her stomach. It was brown, and so smooth and round it was like velvet. I had not felt flesh as young as this for a very long time.

Her stomach gurgled faintly—the girl, understandably, was nervous. I reached up and cupped both her breasts in my hands. They were full and firm, the nipples erect. I placed one in my mouth and sucked it vigorously, seeking nourishment, comfort, release. She moaned, and placed both her hands on my shoulders.

She was too shy, too overcome by my presence, to do anything herself. I understood this, so I took one of her hands and placed it on my throbbing organ. There was a sharp intake of breath. I wondered if I was much larger than Mohammed, more than she was used to? I believed this was likely.

I could contain myself no longer. I lifted my robe, thrusting my hips forward on the chair as I did so, my palm tree pointing boldly towards the roof of the cave. I wanted her to look at it, admire it, possibly even comment on its impressive dimensions, but she kept her eyes averted.

She straddled me, one hand on my shoulder, the other guiding my palm tree towards her oasis. For just a second she let the tip of my organ play at her entrance, and then she thrust downwards so that the whole of my length penetrated deep inside her, probably to the very mouth of her womb.

She let out a squeal as she did so and I, unable to contain myself any longer, let out a mighty cry: "O scourge of the West! O slayer of infidels! O wooer of Laura!" And I who had not known a woman for many, many weeks, possibly even months, bestowed upon this humble maidservant her reward for doing Allah's wishes, blessed her with my essence, pumped her full of my deity, throbbed and pulsed within her for what must have seemed to her like an eternity.

I can still see the look of surprise in her eyes. I could understand that. She had obviously been overwhelmed. There was a questioning look in her eyes, too, that I felt obliged to answer. "Yes, it is true, my heart belongs to another. Please do not tell anyone of this, not even your husband."

She scrambled off me then, smoothing down her robe, my juices, I imagined, already pouring down her delectable inner thighs. I covered myself. She stood before me, her head down, as if awaiting instructions. She was certainly satiated. I wanted to ask her if I was bigger than Mohammed. Instead I said:

"You may go now. Allah be praised."

"Allah be praised," and she turned and hurried out through the curtains.

I called out her name. She appeared a second later. "Yes, sir?"

"Samah, I would like to see you again, if Mohammed, may God protect him, is in agreement."

"Yes, sir, of course, sir," and she went out again.

I hoped she wouldn't boast to everyone about our afternoon of pleasure. I wanted it to remain our secret.

January 25.

Bitterly cold. Go around wrapped in every piece of clothing I own.

My computer whiz, Fazul, has released a computer virus, the SQL Slammer Worm, on the world, and brought internet traffic almost to a halt throughout the US, Europe and Asia. He won't tell me what else he's planning—"It's too early to talk about it yet, Os"—but promises to reveal all soon. Although he added that I probably won't be able to understand what he's doing! I find this unlikely.

February 2.

Am writing to Mark Burnett, Executive Producer of *Survivor* at CBS and suggesting that the next series be filmed out here, on the Afghanistan/Pakistan border. To hell with tropical islands, the Australian outback, Africa, the Amazon and pussy places like that. This will really sort the men from the boys.

The big prize will be capturing me—ha, ha! It will save CBS a lot of money because, should anyone succeed in their mission, then they can collect the $25 million reward money from the US Government—which makes the current $1 million prize money look like peanuts. But the big change in the program will be that contestants will be able to be bumped off by me and my men. That will be the challenge for them, the ultimate test: to survive my al-Qaeda militia. (I guess contestants will have to be given some kind of weaponry to even things out: maybe an AK47 or something, plus ammo every day.)

It will be the ultimate reality TV show. Viewing figures will just skyrocket, and my fame will be truly global—at last! So long as CBS is willing to sign confidentiality agreements and safety guarantees, then I would be happy to sit on a special Tribal Council and vote on who is out of the game at the end of the week.

(We'd have to make sure we didn't shoot all of the contestants on the first day. Restrict ourselves to just one a week maybe.)

February 11.

My latest videotape hits the West—no, the world. Let's not misunderestimate (as Bush would say) its importance.

In it I stressed that it was the duty of all Muslims to resist US forces should they choose to invade Iraq—which I know they will. Bush has wanted to invade Iraq ever since his Daddy got fucked over by Saddam.

I wonder if my sons would do something like that for me. I can't see it somehow.

February 21.

I dreamt of Laura last night. I have not dreamt of her for some time now. This morning I awoke most unsettled, as if everything had been left in the air, undecided.

In the dream, it was she who made the first move, and it was I who tried to hold her back. She was wearing a chambermaid outfit and cleaning round one of the caves with Clorox when she suddenly came across to me and kissed me tenderly on the lips. Immediately I was aroused. But other people were present. I don't know who they were or what they were doing there, because they kept very much in the background. But I felt they were watching us, and George could have been amongst them, so I pushed her away.

How could I have been so stupid? It may only have been a dream, but to push her away like that, to spurn my love, it is unbelievable.

I shall try and have the same dream again tonight, and this time I won't push her away. This time I'll make sure I plant my palm tree.

March 1.

I looked at myself in the mirror this afternoon. Most days I look at myself in the mirror, but today I took a longer look.

I hate my fat lips. They're really fat. They're definitely my worst feature, I'm sure of it. They're too full—I think that's the word they use: full. They look like a woman's lips. I'm sure some people just look at them and want to kiss me.

If I had thinner lips—not exactly non-existent ones, just thinner—I think I'd look stronger and more determined. It would make people take me more seriously. People take me seriously now, especially in the West, but I mean *really* seriously. People respect thin lips, I've noticed that. You don't mess around with someone who has thin lips.

My eyes are good though. I think they're my best feature. I can see a quiet dignity in there, with just a hint of innocence and idealism. And they're nicely set off by my well-defined eyebrows.

But I noticed that my beard is beginning to go gray. There are streaks here and there, nothing too serious, but it is definitely becoming noticeable. Next time Omar or one of the others goes into town I think I'll ask them to get me some Grecian 2000. I'm sure they'll all be quick to have a laugh at my expense, but I'll explain to them that it's not good if people think I'm too old for this game. I have to look young and dynamic. It's also important that I appear relaxed and at ease, not like someone who's on the run from the world's mightiest army—even if I am.

My nose I'm definitely worried about. I think it makes me look Jewish. God forbid! I keep that to myself, obviously. I never even hint of that to anyone, not to anyone.

No one's ever said anything about me looking Jewish, so perhaps it's just my imagination. Perhaps I'm being over-sensitive. But imagine if people thought the head of al-Qaeda looked like a Jew, imagine the scandal.

Sometimes I worry that people think I look Jewish, and are just not saying anything—or only saying it to each other, which would be even worse.

"Have you noticed anything about Os?"

"What's that?"

"Don't you think, sometimes, he kind of looks a little, well, *Jewish*?"

"Funny you should say that…"

I'm not vain. I don't want anyone to think I'm vain. I can look at my face quite objectively. I'm just interested in it, not admiring it or anything like that. Having said that, I don't think I'm ugly. In fact, I think I look quite striking at times. My right profile's particularly good. And Allah be praised for that.

March 4.

They have captured Khalid Shaikh Mohammed in Pakistan. I'm worried about what he will tell them. Certainly the Americans will be keen to get their hands on him. Of course, the enemy is building it up already, saying that the man is one of the most important al-Qaeda operatives, how our organization will now be severely weakened, blah, blah, blah. It pisses me off. It's simply not true. The man's an idiot. I'm the only indispensable one around here.

What worries me is that Khalid will tell everyone it was he who conceived of and directed the 9/11 attacks. I know the man: arrogance is his middle name. That would make me ill if he tried to steal the glory that is rightly mine from under my very nose. I have heard how he has boasted of being the brains behind the operation before, and yet his contribution was so insignificant. I did it all— with a little help from Ayman, of course, but only a little.

Maybe I can get Khalid assassinated. I shall have a word to Ayman. It is in both our interests after all.

March 7.

It wasn't exactly like a real Western because we were both wearing black. From what I understand of the Western conventions, one of us should have at least had a white hat. I was wearing a black kufiyya and agal(2) with a black robe, which is most unusual as I always wear white. He wore a black cowboy outfit with a black Stetson. We were standing—both "standing tall,"—in the dusty main street of a deserted town, and I think there was even tumbleweed in the distance. Bushy drew his gun and fired, but I never moved. Everything was in slow motion, and very dramatic. Bullets were flying around me, but I was unharmed. I was quite unfazed by being shot at, very calm. After what seemed like an age, he had to reload. That was when I drew my revolver. However, before I could fire, I woke up. It was a very strange dream.

March 8.

Every newspaper I open, every television station I watch, every radio station I tune into, it is all about weapons of mass destruction and Saddam Hussein. I'm sick of it. He's getting much more media coverage than me.

Who cares if Saddam has WMDs, that's what I want to know? He would never dare use them, not with Israel on his doorstep.

Anyway, I don't believe he does have them; that's what I've been told. I think he's bluffing the Americans. It's a dangerous game if he is, and I cannot work out what his motive is for doing so. The man is an idiot, a waste of skin, so maybe he doesn't have a motive. That is more than likely.

All this talk of WMDs makes me restless. It even stops me sleeping at night. I want some WMDs, even just one. If I had a WMD, I'd make better use of it than that jumped-up dictator.

Meanwhile, there are protests against the Iraq war in every major city in the West. The people are able to see the stupidity of the invasion, so I'm lucky their governments cannot. Are only the mentally defective elected to government?

March 10.

Happy birthday to me, happy birthday to me, happy birthday dear Osama…No one remembered the importance of the date, of course. I had to remind everyone, but it was too late for them to buy me anything. They are all so selfish and self-involved. Luckily, I am a typical Piscean: compassionate, kind, selfless, sympathetic, gentle, patient and idealistic, even unworldly, so I was able to forgive them—although it was something of a struggle to be so magnanimous.

I had visions of Samah tying a ribbon round her thighs and letting me open them, but it was not to be. She, too, can be quite thoughtless, whereas it would have been so easy for her to have acted charitably towards me.

March 12.

Phoned the Person Of Restricted Growth in the khaki windbreaker and congratulated him on firing another missile into the Sea of Japan and upsetting the Americans. But also suggested he might stop wasting his valuable missiles by splashing them into the ocean and instead fire them across the DMZ into South Korea, or even further afield, at Japan or Australia—depending on how far he can get them to go. They're probably fueled by rice or something, if I know him. He told me he is "playing velly clever game that you do not understand, Mr. Laden." I most certainly don't. He must have a different view of the world being only five foot tall.

March 16.

Tonight, Abu and I are in a cave near the Shera Shing Pass on the Afghanistan-Pakistan border. Because there are only fifteen command centers in the mountains, some in Pakistan and some in Afghanistan, it's not always possible to spend the night in one. The distance between them can be too great to cover in a day. That's when we spend the night in a cave or under canvas.

I prefer the command centers or bunkers because they're set up with all mod cons. Some of them are quite luxurious. One or two even have central heating systems installed. They all have lighting, rudimentary kitchens, some furniture and enough room for up to one hundred men and a few horses. Many are situated several hundred yards back into the mountain, and comprise a series of caves, all interlocking.

Only Ayman and I know the whereabouts of all the command centers, although Abu is always with me, so I guess he does too. I am gambling on the fact that he's so thick he won't have made a mental note of their various locations. The idea is that if anyone is captured and tortured by the Americans, they won't be able to disclose too much, simply because they won't know too much.

The cave I'm in tonight is like an emergency bolt hole: more basic than a command center. It hasn't been excavated at all, and yet it is still quite large. Only bare necessities are stored here: survival rations for three or four men for a week, some wood for a fire, and blankets for warmth at night. These caves can still be very cold.

I don't like spending the night in a cave or a tent, and always try not to do so, but sometimes it cannot be avoided. The main reason for my dislike is that security is less tight than in one of the command centers, so Abu insists on sleeping right next to me—almost on top of me if the truth be told.

Abu is big and dumb (this is me being totally objective, if anything a little kind), and I suppose that's what makes him such a great bodyguard. He is excessively loyal; he really would lay down his life for me without a moment's hesitation. Sadly, he won't take no for an answer.

I'll say—and I do say every time I find myself in this predicament: "Thank you, Abu, you may go to bed now. I will stay up for awhile and pray."

However, he will choose to sit there, like some devoted pet, waiting for me to finish my prayers. The fact is, I rarely pray on these occasions, being far too busy working out a stratagem for getting rid of this well-meaning gorilla so that I won't have to lie right next to him.

I don't wish to offend him: his loyalty is too valuable for that, and it's likely that one day I will be obliged to call on him to lay down his life on my behalf. So I have to keep on the right side of him. It's like keeping an insurance policy up to date.

I pretend to pray, while keeping a weather-eye on the giant sitting watching me from a few feet away. He is like a dog sitting next to the table while his master eats, hoping that a morsel will come his way. He has exactly the same expression on his face.

I always drag my prayers out for as long as possible in the hope that he'll become impatient and go off to bed by himself. Once I prayed for over an hour, but it was still to no avail. Eventually I will sigh deeply, which Abu doubtless takes to be the conclusion of a long and intimate discourse between myself and Allah, but which is in fact me resigning myself to spending another night in close proximity to him. And I will say: "Oh you shouldn't have bothered to stay up, Abu."

"That's all right, boss."

"Let us retire then."

Retirement consists of listening to him snore. He snores loudly and enthusiastically. He also smells. But no, he does not smell, he *stinks*. He stinks of sweat, of goats, of farts and of feet—the latter, I would guess, not having been washed for a very, very long time; probably months. If I was to say that it is like sleeping next to an animal, I would be denigrating animals.

The truth is, when Abu sleeps next to me, I don't sleep at all. I toss and turn all night. I try to cover my nose with the sleeve of my robe, I bury my head beneath the blanket, I turn my back on the offending object, but still I am unable to shut my eyes. Sometimes I think of Laura and surreptitiously stroke the palm tree in the hope that it will tire me and so help me sleep. But I don't get much enjoyment out of this because I'm forever worrying that Abu is not really asleep and can hear me partaking of this nefarious practice.

At other times I will try and remind myself how Allah would behave towards my bodyguard if He was in my position, but am unable to imagine Him being any more charitable than I am myself. Surely He would be unable to put up with either the stench or the noise. I end up persuading myself that it is more than reasonable for me to have these feelings of nausea and disgust.

When all else fails, I push the sleeping giant away from me, propelling him as far as I am able across the floor of the cave with both my hands and feet.

Often even this does not wake him up. But when it does, he scrabbles for his Kalashnikov, muttering, "Who's there? Halt! Give me the password." All mixed with various swear words. Fuck, can he swear!

I pretend to be asleep, so that should he suspect me of having pushed him off his blanket, he will at least think I did it unconsciously. The problem is, this maneuver always ends up in the same way: Abu will lie back down again, curling up like a contented beast at the feet of his master, but invariably closer to me than he was before. I gnash my teeth while my nostrils are again assailed, and try to turn my mind off from the torment.

March 18.

Bush is so keen to invade Iraq, but 30 odd years ago he wasn't so keen to invade Vietnam—or not personally. He managed to side-step that one pretty neatly, joining the almost-impossible-to-get-into National Guard instead. (Just listen to Daddy pulling and yanking on those strings in the background!) There was no way George was going to end up as cannon fodder, although he doesn't seem to worry so much about who becomes cannon fodder today.

Laura calls him "Bushy." How sickening is that. Makes him sound like some bushy-tailed, cuddly gray squirrel—the kind that bites your nuts.

March 20.

Dear diary, what a day!

The infidels have invaded Iraq, and are already storming across the country. "Shock and Awe" they call it. I refuse to be impressed, despite the images being played again and again on my satellite TV.

One night the Americans dropped one thousand precision-guided missiles and bombs on the city, reducing countless buildings to rubble. It's been reported they didn't mean to hit some of those buildings, but hey, that's precision bombing for you.

They have also launched a major offensive (they've called it Operation Valiant Strike—who comes up with these names; some retired cleaning lady at the Pentagon?) in the south of Afghanistan, about sixty miles east of Kandahar. Apache and Black Hawk helicopters have blasted my men in the Sami Ghar mountains.

Luckily, I'm safe up in the north east, well out of trouble.

Worst news of all, Pakistani forces have arrested two of my boys near Rabat. "Bin Laden's sons captured!" is of course screamed by all their newspapers. I'm not too worried; it will toughen them up.

What terrifies me is their grandmother finding out. Doubtless she will hear, eventually, and I shall receive a summons to call her.

March 21.

I read the Sunday edition of the New York Times every week, but often don't get it until the middle of the week. Sometimes it comes out with a pastrami sandwich from the Carnegie Deli. I just love that. Mind you, it can be pretty stale by the time it arrives, but it's better than nothing.

One day, however, I intend to go to the Carnegie Deli on 55th and 7th in person, probably on a sunny Saturday or Sunday morning, and queue up with the locals for my bagels, cream cheese and lox. Or maybe their gefilte fish—quite magnificent. And certainly their cheesecake, topped with blueberries. Yum! And I'll enjoy my treat while sitting at a table reading the weekend edition of the New York Times *on the weekend*. So it will be a double treat. And I won't let all the Jews around me ruin my day. I'll try and ignore them, despite the fact they will be, I'm sure, their usual loud and opinionated selves.

March 22.

Crazy Cheney has won. He did everything bar declare war himself to get the US to invade Iraq. Halliburton, his old company, is said to be making around $8 billion in contracts through this invasion, and Cheney is rumored to be still receiving money from them. He may be crazy, but he's clever too. This is the man who in the past was more than happy to do business with Saddam Hussein, Iran and Qaddafi. Truth is, he'll do business with anyone if there's a dollar in it for him. He'll even send his country off to war if it'll make him some money. They say he has absolutely no empathy with his fellow man, none at all. The only thoughts and feelings he can identify with are his own. He obviously doesn't have my sensitivity.

Talking of which, my piles have returned with a vengeance.

April 9.

Baghdad has fallen to the Americans. One nasty piece of work has been substituted by another. They toppled some giant statue of Saddam in the center of town, and everyone thought this was very symbolic. But they haven't found the man himself. They haven't toppled him; he has disappeared.

Now the Americans have Osama bin Laden and Saddam Hussein running around the world causing havoc, and George W. is pretending everything is fine and dandy and completely under control. It's a right little game of hide and seek.

"Where is that man, Osama bin "Will-o'-the-Wisp" Laden?"

What fun we are all going to have.

April 12.

Yesterday Ayman and I decided to make another video. It's something I enjoy doing, not just because it's a welcome break from routine, but because it's fun putting the fear of God into all our enemies in the West—which, let's face it, isn't too difficult to do. It's always a good way of taunting them, too. Allah be praised!

I actually think many westerners look forward to our new video release, maybe not as much as they look forward to a new George Clooney or Brad Pitt film, but with a real sense of excitement and anticipation nevertheless. They're interested to hear what I've been doing. I sometimes imagine them asking each other at mealtimes, "Hey, Hank, what's Osama bin up to? Patsy, you had any news of Osama recently? Anyone know how he's getting along?" People do care—more than one thinks. That's what my nanny always said to me (she was usually trying to reassure me about my Dad.)

Last night we worked on the script. It was full of the usual stuff: about the decadence of the West, the invasion of Iraq, the plight of the Palestinians (not that I really give a fuck about them), and the evil empires of Israel and America. I do get bored going over the same ground again and again, but Ayman, who fancies himself as a bit of a strategist, insists that we keep plugging away at these points.

"They have short attention spans in the West," he told me. "They're not like us. Do you know that during their election campaigns, politicians have to go in for what they call 'sound bites'?"

It turns out that these are one or two sentences, ideally attached to some strong, memorable image that can be slotted into the evening news on TV. "That's all the general public are able to assimilate. It's said that the average television viewer in America has the attention span of a two year old. Can you believe that?"

We both thought this very amusing, if only because it confirmed what we believed already—especially about George W. It also gave me the idea of introducing a sound bite into my talk in an attempt to beat them at their own game. Ayman thought this an excellent idea.

I came up with a couple of good sound bites this evening. We were alone, having told everyone else to go and sit outside and keep out of our way.

"But it's freezing outside," Hassan protested. He's a weaselly little man and always complaining about something. I have no idea how he made it through basic training.

"It doesn't matter. Get out there anyway. This is secret stuff Ayman and I are doing. Men's business."

The first sound bite I came up with was: "The lumbering superpower is crumbling." I thought that had a real resonance about it, especially the "umb" in both the second and the fifth words. Ayman wasn't as impressed as me. "It's OK," he said, without much enthusiasm.

I insisted: "That's the kind of memorable sentence they'll all be quoting on the sidewalks of New York in a week or two. It'll catch on, Ayman, believe me."

He wasn't persuaded, but he let me keep it in my speech nevertheless. The other line I came up with was, "Oil will cause the West to slip up; oil will bring them to their knees."

I thought that was clever, a nice play on words, although Ayman suggested it was a little too contrived. I think he was just jealous, so we left that in as well.

This morning the weather was fine and sunny. There is still plenty of snow up near the summits, but further down the mountains flowers are beginning to appear. Spring has truly arrived and it is the perfect time for filming.

After breakfast, I suggested that the four of us (myself, Ayman, Abu and Mohammed, who is going to operate the camera), head across to the next valley, in the direction of Pirsirai. It was a half hour walk, but I liked the terrain there. "There's a stream and some big boulders that will form an interesting backdrop."

"There's a stream and some big boulders in every valley," said Mohammed, who is another one who always finds something to complain about, and is basically very lazy. He never likes to walk anywhere. He's so lazy he's been known to pee in the cave, in front of everyone, rather than walk a few yards outside.

"What's the big deal about the stream and the boulders in the next valley, Os?" he asked.

"There's something different about them. I believe it will allow for a dynamic interplay between sunshine and shadow. The effect could be quite Wellesian," I added, keen to demonstrate my knowledge of film history. "*A Touch of Evil*, remember?" Neither of them did. "Anyway, the sun will be at the right angle."

I regard these videos of mine, not just as political statements, but as filmic statements. I would like them to survive in their own right, as works of art. The others are too crass to appreciate this.

Location is extremely important to our short films: it sets the mood and can subconsciously affect the viewer's perception of the whole. Ayman and I appreciate this. The dialogue and direction (if you can call what Mohammed does, direction) should not be ignored, but we know that it is the location that's pored over by the FBI and CIA and hundreds of film experts in the US as soon as our films are released. Our location is studied more closely than the latest celluloid effort from Hollywood's hottest director. They painstakingly examine and analyze every rock, blade of grass and rivulet of water in the hope that it will disclose our hiding place. But we are too clever for them.

The fact is, every valley looks much the same in these parts, one mountaintop much the same as the next, and it would be astonishing if anyone could deduce where we are hiding from one of these short videotapes. Especially when I always insist that Mohammed films us in tight, so as to reveal very little of the background. We avoid the panoramic.

I put on my best robe—my Sunday robe—when I got up this morning. I also combed my hair and beard, and took special care wrapping my turban around my head. I spent a good half hour in front of the small mirror above my bunk: I wanted to look good. This can be hard to achieve when you don't have a full length mirror.

Ayman, I couldn't help noticing, had taken similar care with his appearance. I know how important these cameo appearances are to him, and that he really puts his heart and soul into them. He normally just has a walk-on part (more like a sit-in part, as a matter of fact), although I do sometimes give him a few words to say.

This came about because he once confessed to me that if our bid for world domination eventually came to nothing and al-Qaeda fell apart, then he might try his luck in Bollywood.

"I believe I'm a natural actor, Osama," he said to me—rather theatrically I thought, stressing the "*or*" of actor quite unnecessarily.

I'm not so sure. I can see him acting the part of a vampire, maybe, or a rapist. Possibly a serial killer, but not Hamlet. However, the film world would be an excellent place for him as it is full of sexual deviants.

One of the reasons I'm a little reluctant to give him anything to say is because I know he'll be up all night, pacing the length of the cave, rehearsing his one line, keeping everyone awake. It could be just a sentence or two but he'll treat it like a major soliloquy from Shakespeare.

Sometimes it's more than I can bear, watching his breathing exercises, his clearing of the nasal passages, the way he will dramatically throw his arms around when he is saying something as simple as, "We will throw the Americans out of Iraq." He told me that when he was young he saw Olivier on stage in London, and I suspect he models himself on that gentleman.

It didn't take long to walk to the next valley, although Mohammed moaned the whole way. I don't know why, because Abu was carrying everything as usual: the camera, tripod and a change of wardrobe for me should it be required. Like a packhorse, Abu never complains.

"What on earth's the matter?" Ayman shouted at Mohammed at one point. "Abu's carrying everything for you. What more do you want?"

"I'm carrying the cassettes. Osama isn't carrying much; he could take the cassettes. He hasn't got a sore leg like me." He regarded me slyly from beneath lowered brows.

I should have stayed above such petty squabbling, but couldn't resist saying: "I'm praying. I can't be expected to carry lots of things and pray as well."

After that, Mohammed followed us in silence, his limping suddenly more pronounced. He was sulking.

I was carrying quite enough: my trusted Kalashnikov, which I had captured off the Russians when they retreated from Afghanistan in 1989. I hadn't in fact captured it (a confession for these pages only.) One of my men shot a retreating Russian soldier in the back, and I rushed forward and grabbed the rifle off the ground before he was able to reach it. He was furious when I claimed the trophy for myself, but I pretended not to see him, and he didn't dare argue.

A bit of an aura has built up around this weapon over the years, even if I say so myself. It has become something of an icon. We have included it in every video we've made so far. It enjoys a kind of guest appearance.

"It looks great, Osama," Ayman always says to me. "It makes you look like a real warrior, the fighting prophet, you know the kind of thing."

"Like an avenging angel?"

"Exactly. That's it exactly. Like an avenging angel. I like it."

So it's now included in all our videos without any discussion.

The only discussion we still have, every time we make a video, is what we should do with it. Should I be holding the rifle in a relaxed manner, across my knees for instance, or should I have it leaning casually against the side of my leg in an upright position? The other option is to have it leaning against a rock face in the background of the shot, carefully positioned in frame.

There are arguments for both approaches.

If I hold the Kalashnikov, viewers will hopefully get the impression that I have just this second stopped fighting the Americans, and am grabbing a quick break to speak to freedom fighters around the world. They'll think I'm going to be on my way again very shortly, back at the front, fighting the good fight, gun blazing.

This is very much the hands-on approach. If we had the technical ability to get smoke to come from the end of the barrel for this scenario, we would do that, too. We could make it look as if the Kalashnikov was red hot from use. I could maybe even fire a few rounds out of frame as I spoke, as if I was holding the infidel at bay. But that might be overdoing it.

The other option is to use the rifle as a background prop. To viewers this will hopefully look as if I'm totally relaxed about the war with the West, so at ease in fact, I do not even bother to keep my trusted weapon close at hand, "at the ready." I know no fear, that's what it says having my Kalashnikov leaning casually in the background against a rock face. There's a nice degree of understatement about such an approach.

Of course, as someone once pointed out, if I'm seen holding the Kalashnikov, some people might take it that I'm worried the Americans are about to appear over the horizon and attack. They might interpret this visual statement along these lines: Osama bin Laden is frightened and wants to be ready to defend himself. Apart from being a blatant lie, that certainly would not be a good message to put out there.

In fact something like that almost happened about a year ago. We had started filming a new video, when there was an almighty roar, an explosion of sound, and an American F111 screamed straight up the valley from Asal Karez, about twenty meters off the ground, passed us before we even heard it, rocketed vertically up over the 2,800 meter summit behind us, and disappeared. I thought I was going to have a heart attack.

Luckily, the pilot hadn't seen us—I doubt he had seen anything he was going so fast—and after recovering from our shock, we continued to film. But I sometimes wonder if the CIA or FBI or whoever looks at these things, when they analyzed that particular video of ours, noticed the tremor in my hands, and the uneasy look in my eyes. I believe my eyes in that video looked very nearly as shifty as Bush's. But then his are like that all of the time.

When we reached the next valley, while Mohammed set up the camera, I went through the script, rehearsing it a final time. I always try to make my delivery look unrehearsed: spontaneity somehow conjures up sincerity, makes people think that I really believe what I'm saying. Not only are there subtle nuances in the setting of these films, but also in what I say and how I say it. I would definitely put myself up for an acting Oscar if I thought the judging could be considered in any way impartial.

Ayman had picked out a suitable boulder on which, or against which, he and I could sit. I told him I wanted to put some mud on my face. "It'll make me look like a real terrorist."

"You don't need props like that, Osama. It will simply make you look like a common fighter."

"A fighter of the people, but that's what I am."

"You're above all that, Osama. If anyone has mud on his face, it should be me. I am the fighter."

"I'm more of a fighter than you," I protested. "How many Russians did you kill in Afghanistan?"

"A lot."

"That's not what I heard."

"Oh yes, and what did you hear?" His voice had dropped ominously low. I thought I should be careful.

"Nothing much. But I myself shot many hundreds."

"Did you now?"

"I cannot be exact, but many hundreds it would have been. Possibly thousands."

"I don't believe you." I could barely hear him now. It was a bad sign.

"It's true!"

"Liar!" He hissed the word at me, spittle catching on the strands of beard around his mouth. I was stunned by such blatant aggression.

"Liar yourself," I said feebly.

For a few minutes neither of us spoke. I was furious. How dare he stop me putting mud on my face. It would make me look tough. I reached into my pack and took out a bottle of Valium; I swallowed two pills.

Mohammed, oblivious to our little contretemps, was whistling away to himself as he set up the tripod. Abu was reclining on the grass nearby. He gave me a cheerful thumbs up. He can always tell when I'm upset. Briefly I pondered the possibility of getting him to beat up Ayman. Then my deputy suddenly decided to try and make up with me. He was probably worrying about his film career going down the gurgler.

"Osama, look, let's not fight over this. We don't have the time to argue about such a small matter. All I'm saying—and I've said it to you many times before—is that you are the prophet. You are the wise man of peace—"

"Peace!?" I screamed at him. "*Peace!!*"

Out of the corner of my eye I saw Abu sit up and grab his rifle.

"Relax, Osama, relax. Take it easy. Keep your turban on. Yes, peace. You are waging this war reluctantly. You mustn't forget that. I don't care how much you enjoy playing guerillas—and I know how important it is to you—but you have to remember you're doing it reluctantly."

"And why's that, *Teacher*?" I was trying to sound sarcastic when I called him Teacher. I know he hates to be called that; it reminds him of the past.

"The only reason you fight is because of the brutality of the Americans. They force you to take up arms. They have invaded our lands, they have desecrated the shrines and holy sites of Islam, they have raped our women and plundered our homes. You have taken up arms in order to protect Muslims around the world, to save us from the evil and profanity of the American infidel."

He was persuasive. "Yes, OK, I do sometimes forget that," I said grudgingly.

"I know how it is, brother. But it's important you don't forget. That is why your films are so good."

I could tell he was trying to butter me up now, and I briefly wondered why. He was holding a blade of grass between his two thumbs and trying to whistle. It wasn't working. He threw the grass away.

"What's so great about your films, Osama, is the modest way you keep your eyes lowered, the humble way you sit out in the countryside, amongst nature, the lack of fake props."

"I have my Kalashnikov."

"That is not a prop. That is real. That is you. And what's so great about the Kalashnikov is that it provides a brilliant contrast to your wise and gentle smile. You have the smile of a philosopher, of a wise man, and you have the weapon of a killer. It's great stuff, Osama. I love it! Keep it. Play the sincerity bit for all it's worth. You'll have the viewers eating out of your hand."

"You think so, Ayman?" I was almost convinced.

"I know so. You don't look like a terrorist. I'm sorry to disappoint you," he added, seeing my crestfallen face, "but that is your strength. The fact you don't look like a guerilla is a big plus. You look like a man of peace. Like I have said to you before, many times, you look like Jesus Christ."

"But I don't want to look like Jesus Christ, for Chrissake!"

"Well, that's tough, because you do. And that will really get up their noses. It's great, it's exactly what we want. That's what we need, you to look like Jesus Christ."

He crouched beside me. "You know what, if I could get my hands on some little kids to play at your feet while you spoke, maybe a little girl to sit on your lap, now, that would be something else. Imagine that. Uncle Osama surrounded by innocent little children. The world would love you for that."

"Well, surely you of all people know how to get your hands on innocent little children?" I couldn't help myself.

"Let it go, Osama," he said, his voice suddenly dropping several decibels.

I decided it was best to move away from that particular subject. "But do we want people in the West to open their hearts to me?" I was a little uncertain as to what he was proposing.

"Some of them we do, absolutely. It would be great if a few people in the world loved you. Not many, but a few."

He stood up and went across to speak to Mohammed, and I tried to think myself into the part. I closed my eyes and practiced my breathing techniques. Method acting, that was what was required here; a touch of the Marlon Brando's. A bit of mumbling and muttering would definitely not go amiss.

I knew it was all up to me. Ayman would be sitting beside me but, apart from a smile every now and again, and the odd shake or nod of the head, he wouldn't be saying anything in this video. The responsibility was all on my shoulders.

"Mohammed's ready," said Ayman. I opened my eyes. He was blocking my sun.

"Is this my best profile?" I shouted across the clearing to Mohammed.

"I don't know," he answered petulantly. I could tell he was still sulking because we'd made him carry the cassettes. "Which is your best profile, anyway? I'm sure I don't know."

Ayman interrupted us. "It's your best profile, Osama. Don't worry. Relax."

"Have you focused?" I asked Mohammed. "Make sure we're in focus, not like the last time."

"That wasn't my fault. There was something wrong with the camera."

My deputy raised his eyes to the sky and muttered, "Allah, spare me from this idiot."

I wondered why these sessions were always so fraught. They should be enjoyable.

"Take one, scene one," shouted Mohammed across the clearing.

"There is only one scene, Mohammed."

"I know that, but that's what they say."

"Forget it, Osama. Let the idiot have his fun."

I shrugged.

Mohammed shouted: "Take one, scene one. Roll camera, and...action!"

I made my speech, or gave my little talk as I prefer to call it, and afterwards Ayman leapt to his feet, grabbed my hand and shook it enthusiastically. "Osama, that was great. Great! Mohammed, wasn't that great?"

There was silence from Mohammed. Ayman stared at him, his eyes narrowing suspiciously. "I said, wasn't that great, Mohammed. What do you think? Was it great?"

"I thought it was a rehearsal. I thought you were doing a rehearsal."

"But you said 'Take one, scene one' and all that other bullshit, and now you tell me you weren't even filming."

"I was rehearsing too. I thought it was a rehearsal for both of us."

I had to restrain Ayman. I saw him look briefly at Abu as if contemplating a change of cameraman, but just as quickly dismiss the thought. If there had been anyone else around capable of operating the camera, I think Ayman would have quite happily killed Mohammed right then and there. And I might have been tempted to join in. If only Michael Moore had been around.

I did my speech again.

"Os, that was great," said Mohammed without much sign of conviction after I'd finished. And Abu applauded enthusiastically from his position on the grass.

"And you filmed it that time, you yak-brained idiot?" Ayman asked pleasantly. Mohammed didn't answer him, just nodded.

"We have a wrap," shouted Ayman, and danced a little jig. He started huffing almost immediately, and was forced to stop. "We'll get that off to *El-Jazeera* first thing tomorrow morning. Then sit back and watch the fun," he panted.

I laughed and slapped him on the back. All of a sudden I felt quite good-natured. At times I almost liked the man.

April 13.

Dreamt of Laura again last night. This time I planted my palm tree in her oasis. It was memorable. We did it on a pile of returned library books.

April 28.

Got really excited today—much too excited for my health, to be honest—when CNN announced Dick Cheney's death. But no sooner had I cracked open a bottle of bubbly (the superb—and extremely expensive—vintage 1959 Dom Perignon) and enjoyed a few mouthfuls by myself (unfortunately—ha, ha!—being unable to share such a treat with my brethren, who regularly, and mistakenly, denounce the evils of alcohol), than the announcer came back on screen to apologize and say it had all been a dreadful (sic) mistake!

By then I was in the middle of reminiscing about all the times we had done battle together over the years, and what a superb adversary he had proved to be— you know, being rather magnanimous and generous towards my departed foe, as one often is at such times. Well, I have to say I was a little disappointed when they returned to say that the Vice President is in fact in the pink of condition— apart from his "dicky" heart. I finished off the bubbly nevertheless, now more in the hope of drowning my bitter disappointment.

Cheers, Dick!

April 29.

George W. says he will pull out most of his troops from Saudi Arabia. It's that word *most* that sticks in my throat. He claims some will have to be left behind for the training of Iraqi troops. And if you believe that…He's as slippery as the oil he made his money in.

Anyway, as I explained to Ayman (he hadn't yet managed to work it out for himself), it actually suits us down to the ground. Although we'll complain vociferously about the American presence, it's perfect for us. So long as they stay there, we have an excuse to carry on with our crusade against the invasion of the infidel.

That's what you call tactical thinking.

Weather becoming more bearable by the day.

May 2.

Bush has been filmed on the *USS Abraham Lincoln* making a victory speech about Iraq in his high-pitched voice and using short, staccato sentences as per usual. A big banner hung in the background, fluttering bravely in the breeze: MISSION ACCOMPLISHED it read. I thought I was seeing things when I first set eyes on it, then thought it was some bizarre display of American humor (could they have discovered dramatic irony all of a sudden?), and finally came to the conclusion that my television must be on the blink. But no, sure enough, it was none of those: it was for real. He was all dressed up in some macho flight gear, looking like he was on his way to a fancy dress party.

I wonder who thought that one up: the clown himself or one of his minions.

I must remember to send the world's media a copy of the photograph in ten years time, when the Americans are still trying to extricate themselves from Iraq.

May 10.

I was returning with Abu from a spot of shopping in Chitral in Pakistan, near the Afghanistan border. We drove north for an hour, up the steep, winding road that runs parallel to the border until it becomes little more than a dirt track. I parked the Land Cruiser half a mile outside the tiny village of Owirdeh on a grassy, rock-strewn slope high above Chitral. I got through on my cell phone faster than I expected.

"Hi, George, it's Osama here."

"Osama?" He didn't sound too quick on the uptake.

"Osama bin Laden."

"Aw gee!" he said, or "Aw shucks!" Can't remember which right now. "Would that be the real Osama bin Laden?" he asked.

"Course not, George! I'm just a pretend one."

"Phew, that's a relief. I was fit to be tied for just a moment then." He laughed nervously.

"George," I said, speaking slowly, trying to keep him with me, "yes, it's the real bin Laden."

"Gee, golly gosh. In that case Mr. bin Laden, what can I do for you?"

"You could start by calling me Osama."

"I don't think that's quite proper, considering…"

"Considering what, George?"

"You know, Mr. bin Laden, don't pretend you don't. All folks know. It wouldn't be right to call you Osama."

There was a long silence. I listened to the static on the line.

"Now where exactly would you be calling from, Mr. bin Laden?"

"Chitral."

"I can't say I rightly know Chitral."

"I doubt that you do, George. I understand you never left America until you were President, not once. And you certainly haven't visited Chitral since your election, so I wouldn't think it likely that you do know it."

"To tell you the truth, I never saw much need to travel, not when I live in the best country in the world. So where exactly is this Chitral, Mr. bin Laden?"

"Near the Afghanistan-Pakistan border, about a hundred miles north east of Jalalabad."

"Can't say I know Jalala—Jalala what?"

"Jalalabad."

"Never heard of it."

"It's due east of Kabul, in Afghanistan."

"Don't know that town either. But I've heard it said about Afghanistan that it's a beautiful country."

I said nothing. Just waited.

"Now where exactly in Chitral are you, Mr. bin Laden?"

"In a call box in the market square."

"Am I right in thinking there would only be one call box there?"

"Yes, that's right, George. Just the one. Well done." The truth is there weren't any, but he wasn't to know that.

"Now I get the feeling you're laughing at me, Mr. bin Laden."

"I certainly wouldn't do that. I'd never laugh at a man of your intelligence." I was having problems stifling my laughter.

"Well, that's mighty kind of you to say so. Some folk are mean and say that if you put my brains in a bumblebee, he'd fly backwards."

"Well, I'm not one of them, George."

We exchanged pleasantries for a couple more minutes, when suddenly a Cruise missile streaked overhead, in the direction of Chitral. Three or four seconds later there was an enormous explosion from the market square. Silence, followed by a tentative: "Mr. bin Laden?"

"Yes, George?"

"You still there?" He sounded surprised.

"I'm still here, George."

"Er…in the Chitral market place?"

"No, George, that was yesterday. I was there yesterday, that's what I said: yesterday."

"Ah, is that right? You've got me so every time I stand up, my mind sits down. So where are you now?"

"Me? I'm in a cave near the summit of Tirich Mir."

"Tirich Mir? How do you spell that, Mr. bin Laden?"

I spelt it for him, grinning at Abu as I did so, but of course he didn't have a clue what we were talking about, seeing that we were speaking English. Instead, I pointed out of the window towards the summit of Tirich Mir towering thousands of feet above us. Ali stared upwards, puzzled. Suddenly there was a flash and a cloud of dust and smoke erupted from near the summit. Abu turned towards me, not understanding.

"So how's it all going at your end, George?"

"Is that you, Mr. bin Laden?"

"Of course it is, George. Who else would it be? I thought we'd cleared that particular question up."

"Yes, yes, of course we did. Er…what's it like on Tirich Mir right now?"

"On Tirich Mir? Why do you ask?"

"Oh, I was just wondering, you know."

"Well, I don't know, George."

"But you just told me you were there."

"Did I? Stupid me. I meant to say Nowshack Noshak, not Tirich Mir."

"You're near the summit of Nowshack Noshak?"

"Sure am. And it's a fine view from up here, George. Sure you'd appreciate it if you were here."

"Darn it, Mr. bin Laden, wish I could be with you. Nothing'd give me more pleasure."

I pointed out of the car window in the direction of Nowshack Noshak. This time Abu and I saw the Cruise missile streak across the sky (from the direction of the Persian Gulf, I'd say) and bury itself, with a massive explosion, near the summit.

There was silence on the phone.

"George, I've been pulling your leg. My bad. I'm on the western slope of the peak directly above the village of Parsing, just a couple of hundred feet beneath the summit."

"You promise me, Mr. bin Laden? Not sure that I trust you any more."

"I hope to be kicked to death by grasshoppers if it ain't the truth. Isn't that what you say in Texas?"

I pointed towards the peak above Parsing for Abu's benefit. I felt like a conjurer at a kids' party. Ali was staring open-mouthed as I caused one mountain top after another to explode in flames. I persuaded George to part with four more Cruise missiles before he said: "Darn it, Mr. bin Laden, you're all hat and no cattle. You ain't playing fair with me. I thought I could trust you to at least tell the truth."

"OK, George, I'll tell you where I am."

"Yeah? For real this time?"

"Yes, for real. I'm upstairs in the White House."

"Yeah? Well I never."

"Chatting to Laura."

I could hear him whispering to someone in the background. "He says he's upstairs."

"I don't believe that's possible, Mr. President" was the prompt reply.

I never found out if his Chief of Staff launched a final Cruise missile at the White House, because George suddenly said, "This is nothing but a diarrhea of words and a constipation of thoughts. Good day to you," and slammed the phone down on me. I guess he never did launch that last Cruise missile. If he had, doubtless I would have heard.

May 16.

A bomb goes off in Casablanca café. Nothing to do with me, so I'm not interested. Some upstart organization called al-Assirat al-Moustaquim has claimed responsibility. Who the hell are they? More to the point, who do they think they are? They're copycats, plain and simple, just jumping on the al-Qaeda bandwagon. That's the problem with being a freedom fighter—and something of a trend-setting freedom fighter—every man and his boy thinks they can do it too.

May 20.

I bet Rumsfeld lords it over Bush and Cheney. He wouldn't be able to help himself, rubbing in the fact he did his military service when the other two were out-and-out draft dodgers.

At every opportunity he doubtless says things like:

"Mr. President, when I was in the Navy we used to have a saying…"

Or: "You couldn't be expected to know this, Dick, but on naval exercises in the Pacific, even in mountainous seas you were expected to…"

I can see the two men forcing a smile and nodding while they bite their tongues and try really, really hard not to say what they want to say.

I bet Rumsfeld enjoys that, watching their humiliation.

"I tell you what, Mr. President, a bit of military discipline never did me any harm."

May 29.

Blair visits Iraq, and says: "When people look back at this time and look back at this conflict, they will see it as one of the defining moments of our century."

For the first time ever, I am in complete agreement with the man. It will be seen as the beginning of the end for the corrupt Western powers, the defining moment in their demise.

But he's far too earnest in my opinion, a real Goody-Two-Shoes. Should have stuck to being a choirboy.

June 1.

Bush reminds me of the Dutch tale of the little boy who sticks his finger in the dyke to stop it leaking. Only there are so many leaks in the world dyke right now, and the President just doesn't have enough fingers to go round. What's the little boy in the White House going to do? Stick his palm tree in there, too?

June 16.

I think people are really stupid. A case in point—to prove my theory.

Only six of the nineteen people who died crashing those planes into the twin towers and the Pentagon actually knew they were on a suicide mission. The rest were kept in the dark. They weren't real martyrs, just idiots. They died for the cause, yes, but never knew they were dying for the cause.

What was really stupid is that none of them queried it, none of them asked any awkward questions. "But, Khalid, why are we hijacking a jet if we're not going anywhere?" They just did what they were told, no questions asked.

June 21.

Harry Potter and The Order of the Phoenix, the fifth installment, was released worldwide today. I bet George brushes his teeth, washes his hands and climbs into his pajamas really quickly tonight, so that Mummy Laura can tuck him into bed and read him his favorite story while he sucks away on his thumb. Trouble is, he'll get much too excited, and then he won't be able to sleep, so he'll be like a camel with a sore head tomorrow. And then the whole world will have to look out: which country will Mr. Muggle invade next? Whose oil will he steal? Which little dictator will he kick in the shins in the name of Democracy?

July 1.

My new Nike Air Jordan Retros arrived by special messenger today. Great fit. Now I'll be able to fly across the mountains, defying gravity, like the great man himself. I caught Ali taking a sneaky look at them. Good! I hope he dies of envy.

July 9.

In the cave alone this morning, changing after my wash, when Samah asked through the curtain if she could clean my quarters. Quick as anything I whipped off my towel and stood there as naked as the day I was born. "Yes, Samah, you can come in." Well, she got a real eyeful. But whereas I had hoped the sight of my wonderful torso would put her in the mood for a bit of slap and tickle, it had quite the opposite affect: she screamed and rushed out of the cave. Ungrateful wench.

Women! Can't live with them, can't cut off their heads and make a decent soup.

July 22.

Saddam's two sons, those nasty pieces of work—like father, like sons I always say—have been killed by the Americans in Mosul, in northern Iraq. Good riddance. At times they even managed to make their father look like a good man, and that was some achievement.

July 23.

The BBC claim to have proved the Loch Ness monster does not exist. The rumor is they are now intent on proving the same about me.

July 24.

After another hard afternoon in front of my computer plotting the downfall of the West and the rise of Islam, plus a few games of Battleship and Solitaire, along with a quick check of my favorite porn sites, I stood up and stretched. I needed some fresh air.

I wandered from my private, screened off area into the center of the cave complex. I was several hundred feet underground and at least one hundred yards from the cave entrance that overlooked the Kussa Pass, almost due east of Kandahar. Even a Scud missile would have trouble penetrating this far.

There was no one around. I was surprised, but not in any way alarmed.

They must all be about their various tasks, checking in with the local warlords, tending the animals, and walking up to the summits of the local peaks in order to survey the terrain. I decided to wander outside and see if anyone was around with whom I could pass the time of day.

It took me several minutes to get to the entrance, along a slightly rising path, in a corridor just about a yard and a half wide. I squeezed between two giant rocks, and stepped out into the sunshine. I was temporarily dazzled by the brightness.

It was a glorious afternoon, the sun still high in the sky, but I have to admit that I barely noticed it. Because, as soon as I stopped blinking in the sunlight, I saw, just a few yards from the entrance to the cave complex, the most horrible of sights. Once again, I was dazzled.

Ali was pleasuring a goat in the middle of the grass col. He had the beast on its side, one of his hands clasping its mane, the other pinioning its forelegs, preventing it from getting up and running off which I presumed it would have done had it been free to do so. The animal had its mouth open, and was making pathetic bleating sounds. Its eyes were staring, either with disbelief at what was happening to it or with pleasure caused by the rapid rise and fall of two athletic-looking buttocks. Ali's robe had ridden up around his waist. His buttocks shone resplendent beneath the sun, which gave them a faint yellowish glow. And his headphones were over his ears. Doubtless he was listening to D.J. Vadim's *Terrorist*.

Really, I thought, he could at least have taken the creature over the next rise, out of sight. People don't do this kind of thing on their own front doorstep, at least not where I was brought up.

I coughed, and was ignored. I coughed again, louder. Ali half turned round, barely pausing in his activities. His eyes were glazed, a bit like the goat's. I pondered briefly the possibility of them being in love, but dismissed it out of hand. Ali would only ever fall in love with himself.

He grunted what was possibly a welcome, but may have been no more than an acknowledgement of my presence, then turned back to the business in hand. The goat looked fleetingly towards me for help. It was a look tinged with resignation, as if the animal no longer expected to be rescued by anyone, not even the head of al-Qaeda. I won't say my heart went out to the creature, but I did briefly sympathize with it.

Ali, obviously unfazed by my presence, continued to grunt loudly and grind enthusiastically. He was certainly exerting himself, whether for his own sake or for the sake of the goat or to impress me it was hard to tell. I decided that he was either indifferent to the fact I had walked in on him, or, a far more worrying prospect, was pleased to have a spectator.

I decided I had to do something. "That's disgusting, Ali," I shouted. "It's revolting. Do you hear me? Stop it immediately. I don't believe you're doing something like that."

I could have been a fly that had alighted briefly on his bottom for all the attention he paid to me. "We have to eat that goat, you know," I added plaintively. I didn't want to sound plaintive, but I think I might have come across like that.

I retreated back into the cave. I did not find the thought of sitting looking at the view, while the lovers were enjoying themselves so close at hand, very appealing. There was a foul taste in my mouth, and I had not even started to eat that particular goat. I was very upset. I had heard rumors of Ali's predilection towards our four legged friends, but had preferred to ignore them. Now I no longer could. I had seen the evidence with my own eyes. Those bouncing buttocks were just too hard to ignore.

The thought of that soft white flesh soaked in his sweaty, bodily secretions did not appeal. I'm fond of gravy, but this was just too much. I wondered if I could ask Samah to mark that particular animal, so that when its time came to adorn our table I could stick to yoghurt.

It occurred to me that maybe Ali had had his way with all the goats in our flock. What if that was so? He did not strike me as the faithful sort, a one goat man. He probably liked to play the field! It was more than likely that he had known them all, the whole flock. What could I do then? Not eat goat ever again? But I like it, I love goat. I don't love goat like Ali loves goat, I just love goat like a gastronome. It was too awful to contemplate. He simply shouldn't be allowed to play with his food, *our* food, like that. I would have to speak to someone about him.

I went back to my study area and switched on the television. Hopefully *The Simpsons* would be on. I needed a laugh.

July 26.

I was walking down the bustling main street in the old city of Kandahar today, accompanied as usual by Abu. I was hoping to buy some underpants. At times like this I wish I lived in London and could pop round to the local Marks & Sparks. I'd ignore their Jewish heritage if it meant getting a half decent pair of underpants. I've actually discovered that in our little group only Ayman and I actually wear underpants, which is a rather daunting discovery. Half way down the street, as we stepped around a scarcely moving, overladen cart being dragged by a protesting donkey, we were approached by this little old man. He pointed at me. "I know you."

I smiled pleasantly, and stopped. I confess to these pages alone that I did strike a bit of a pose. The price of fame, I told myself. Abu moved forward, obviously intent on knocking the old man into the gutter. I held up a hand to stop him. After all, it's not every day that one is recognized in the street by a fan.

"Wait a minute," said the old man. "Wait a minute, don't tell me, don't tell me, I know who you are…"

I waited patiently, Abu next to me, clenching and unclenching his fists.

"It'll come to me in a moment, don't tell me." By now the old man was holding onto my robe, obviously keen that I should not escape before he had guessed my identity. "You're…Oh I know you so well! I know, it's that soap they show on Friday evenings, isn't it?"

"You old fool," muttered Abu.

"Or is it Kabul's Wheel of Fortune?"

I was deflated, I have to admit. I decided to put the old man out of his misery. "I'm Osama bin Laden," I told him.

"Oh, yes," the old man shouted, suddenly quite elated, "the singer! You had that hit, *Mujahideeen Blue*."

I interrupted him. "No, not the singer, the freedom fighter. The internationally feared terrorist and scourge of the West."

This time it was the old man who was deflated. "Oh, I thought you were someone important. And to think I was going to ask you for your autograph."

He let go of my robe and continued down the street, a look of disgust on his face.

Abu tried to cheer me up. "Don't worry, boss, the man's obviously escaped from the local lunatic asylum. Imagine not knowing who you are!"

July 27.

We had a fortunate escape today.

Ali was on watch at the cave entrance high up in the Sami Ghar Mountains overlooking Mir Kusha (though it's equally likely he was just fucking one of his goats), when he rushed down to tell us that the Americans were outside. Knowing him and his enthusiasm for mayhem, I am surprised he hadn't taken them on single-handedly. But then maybe his pants had been around his ankles at the time, and he wasn't able to.

We all retreated to the back of the cave, in the pitch black, and crouched there scarcely daring to move, our rifles all pointing towards the entrance. Unfortunately, we were in a cave with only one entrance. There was no way of escape.

We couldn't see the entrance to the cave because the passage did a kind of dog-leg, and it was quite some distance away. I do remember someone farting—I think it was Abu, but he denied it under his breath most vehemently—and all of us being overwhelmed by the smell. Unfortunately, we'd eaten curry the night before.

Then, while we waited, Samah started to giggle. We were all so tense, I think it must have been hysterics. At first we thought she was crying, which would have been more understandable in the circumstances, but when we realized she was laughing, Mohammed whispered to her angrily, and she shut up.

We crouched there in silence, waiting. There was only Ali, Mohammed, Samah and myself. We were traveling from a command center near Nawan, in a north-easterly direction, past Azrow, to a command center near the Khyber Pass. It was a journey of several days. We had known of the cave where we were spending the night, but it was not one of ours.

Finally we heard footsteps coming towards us, from the direction of the entrance, and a man singing. He wasn't singing loudly, more like to himself, almost under his breath. It was a GI and he was alone. He was listening to his Walkman. It sounded like one of those rap songs that are all the craze right now. I caught some of the words, even though we were some distance away. Something about fucking the cops, and the hero shooting his way out of jail. He must have had it up very loud

None of the other soldiers—who were doubtless with him—had obviously considered it necessary to accompany him into the cave. As likely as not they were sitting outside on the grass, smoking cigarettes and enjoying their break in the sunshine. They must have been disappointed by searching so many hundreds of caves, and had probably given up all hope of ever finding us.

The soldier was carrying a torch, and shining it about him in a perfunctory manner. It didn't look as if he expected to find anything out of the usual. Luckily, Allah be praised, he did not shine the torch at us, but instead shone it briefly towards our right, where there was a deep hollow. Then, turning his back to us, he tucked the torch under his arm. It shone directly onto us then as we huddled in the corner of the cave. We were all in the spotlight. We could have been on stage.

He had unzipped his trousers and was relieving himself against the wall of the cave. Samah gasped, quite shocked that a man should do that right in front of her, even though his back was turned towards us and he didn't know we were there. I wanted to point out to her that she was being stupid, that he wouldn't have done something like that if he'd known a woman was present—but then, I'm not so sure about that, not with Americans. He might have been titillated by her presence.

Mohammed quickly put his hand over his wife's mouth. We all stared at each other in the spotlight, horrified by our predicament.

The soldier had a long pee, with us lit up by his torch all the way through it. Finally, he finished, shook himself a few times, sighed and zipped up his trousers. Then, still singing and without turning round, he took his torch in one hand and made his way back out of the cave.

We were all so relieved (ha ha, just like the GI), we leant against each other, grasped each other in congratulatory hugs, and sighed. I felt Samah's breasts momentarily brush against my arm, and I sighed again. I wished she did not belong to Mohammed, and that she could give me comfort, too, like before.

July 28.

Sweet revenge! I only heard it second hand unfortunately. Dearly would I have loved to witness the event for myself.

I sacrificed a remaining half tub of yoghurt in order to trap that thief. I mixed in two desert spoons of salt, and left it in its usual place.

Abu told me several days later, in all innocence, that he thought maybe Ali was sick, because this morning he had risen quickly from where he was sitting on the floor of the cave having breakfast, and had rushed outside. Only he never made it that far: he had thrown up in the passageway leading to the entrance. He had cleaned it up himself. When Abu asked, most solicitously I imagine, if he was all right, Ali had snapped: "Fine, just fine. Must have been something I ate. Forget it, will you." And stormed off.

I don't think I shall have any more worries about my yoghurt supplies.

The weather is glorious. Almost wish I could spend more time outside, in the fresh air, instead of skulking in these caves all day long.

July 29.

Today, we had some good news. The Americans have fucked up big time. They bombed a wedding party in Mullah Omar's house in the Uruzgan Province. They obviously thought he was at home. He wasn't. They managed to kill more than thirty people, many of whom were women and children.

This always makes for good press fodder. The media love it when so-called innocents are killed. They throw their hands up in the air in horror and go totally overboard in the sanctimonious stakes. They're almost as bad as the British when they discover one of their politicians is having extramarital sex. It's quite wonderful to behold.

It's also fun to see US officials on television being grilled about this latest public relations disaster and trying to wriggle out of the deep hole they've dug for themselves. I don't know why they don't just say, "Shit happens," and not bother to try and come up with any explanations. That's what we do in al-Qaeda, and it's much simpler.

July 30

I have a video of what I call the highlights of my career. I tell the others when I play it to them that it is al-Qaeda's highlights. I say this in order to encourage them, but I do not believe it. It is really my highlights. The tape includes footage of the twin towers and the Pentagon, the bombings of the East African embassies, Mombasa hotel, *HSS Cole* and Bali. There are others, but those are the main ones.

I carry one copy of the videotape with me at all times, and keep another copy in a safe house in Kandahar. When I feel I am getting nowhere with my crusade, when I need a little jollying along, that is when I will take it out and watch it.

The problem is, every time I watch this particular videotape I worry. Hitler killed at least six million people. Stalin, some say, killed around twenty million, and Chairman Mao, well, he just went off the dial. I read somewhere, it was 70 million. I am not in the same league. I am small fry compared to them.

A lot of it is luck, really. I mean, most of Mao's 70 million were in China. Imagine if he'd been Chairman in another country—like Australia. No way could he have got up to 70 million. In those days there'd have been about ten million people in Australia. So he bumps them all off, and then what? Maybe he nips across to New Zealand and exterminates all of them, too. But even if he had included all the sheep, he wouldn't have made it past fifteen million. And what if he'd been Chairman of Lichtenstein? He'd have got rid of all his subjects before breakfast. He'd never have made it up to 70 million, that's for sure.

For me, there were around two hundred casualties in Nairobi, ten in Dar es Salaam, approximately three thousand two hundred altogether in New York and the Pentagon, maybe ten thousand Russians in Afghanistan—tops—plus a handful (thirty or forty, say) in car and café bombings here and there. I'd be lucky to get my total up to half a million.

Adolf, Josef and the Chairman would laugh me out of the room. They'd think I was pulling their leg if I told them how many deaths I was responsible for. "Half a million, Os? You've got to be kidding! Or are you just talking last week?"

Having said that, I reckon I'm in more people's heads than those three ever got into—well, maybe not Mao. People lie awake at night all around the world because of me: I am their worst nightmare. Osama bin Laden is their worst night-mare, not Freddy Kreuger.

I'm still not sure I understand why everyone in the West is so terrified of me. According to my files, the Iraqi poison gas attack against the Kurds in 1988 caused between six and eight thousand deaths, and in Srebrenica in 1995 around seven and a half thousand Bosnian Muslims died. And look at the Americans themselves: in the biggest single acts of terrorism ever, they wiped out well over 200,000 civilians in Hiroshima and Nagoya. When you look at figures like that, I'm an innocent. I'm miles behind.

What I need to do is get a nuclear bomb into New York or LA, or London or Paris. Now that would be something else. That would give me a million at least, probably much more. That would propel me straight into the big league, up there with the German, Russian and Chinese dictators. It would be something I could build on. It would certainly make sure my name went down in history—which, of course, is all that interests me. I want to be famous. I want to be men-tioned in the same breath as Stalin, Hitler and Mao.

August 4.

Emailed Blair this morning to ask how he deals with Gordon Brown, his haggis eating deputy. I suspect he has the same problems with Gordon that I have with Ayman, both men forever snapping at our heels like irritating Chihuahuas, and if he can give me any advice as to how to keep my deputy in his place, it will be gratefully received. Little Johnnie Howard Down Under has a similar problem with his deputy I believe, but in that instance the sooner Peter Costello replaces the Prime Minister the better it would be for everyone, so it scarcely seems rele-vant to ask for advice in that quarter. Blair and I are patently different to Little Johnnie in that we are, let's face it, both incomparable and irreplaceable.

On the UK government website, where it invites the public to email the Prime Minister, there is a list of subjects on a drop down menu or you can choose your own. I entered my subject as: "Ensuring one's deputy knows his place." I hope this will stir up sufficient interest to get my email through to the PM.

I was a little cheeky at the end of the email, asking Tony to give Cherie "a big hug and a kiss from me." I wonder if he will? Now that I think of it, should have added "a poke" as well. But then, casting modesty aside, he wouldn't have been as impressive in that department as myself, so maybe it's just as well I didn't ask him to act as my stand in.

August 8.

My bowels have been worrying me. I haven't been regular for a few days now. The truth is, I haven't been at all. I think it's all the meat I've been eating. We're short of vegetables and fruit. Azeem is trying to get some sent up to us, but by the time they arrive I will probably have moved on somewhere else.

This morning, briefly, I thought I felt the urge—only faintly, but there was a distinct possibility of action. I could not afford to pass up the chance, no matter how faint it was. I rushed out of the cave, closely followed by Abu—whose perpetual presence is enough to make anyone constipated.

"You don't have to come with me," I shouted over my shoulder.

"You know I can't leave you, boss."

And that was true enough; he was never allowed to leave my side. I had to put up with him day and night. "Well, sit over there on those rocks and make sure you keep your back to me."

I crouched down on the grass, my robe around my waist, and looked down into the wide valley, carpeted in flowers, that swept all the way to Herat. It was the perfect view for relieving yourself. I strained. I tried to think positive thoughts. My face was burning with the effort. Flies buzzed around optimistically. "No looking!" I shouted across the clearing towards Abu's back. I couldn't feel anything happening. I think rushing out of the cave had made me constipated again.

Then suddenly, without any warning at all, three American F111s streaked past, just a few feet above the ground, appearing from the West, up the valley from the direction of Herat, then disappearing, with an ear-splitting boom, over the Taghman Kah peak behind me, in the east. My heart leapt into my mouth, the mountain shook beneath my feet, and my bowels moved. My bowels really moved.

A series of explosions shattered the peace of the mountains—and, no, it wasn't me! It later transpired the Americans were bombing some empty caves in the next valley, in the direction of Qala Ishlan—they must have received their usual up-to-the-minute data from their spies on the ground about my whereabouts.

Not only did the Americans help me void my bowels, but it was the best movement I had enjoyed for at least a week. With a sigh of pleasure—possibly even gratitude—not unmixed with sheer terror, I felt several days' worth of waste deliver itself onto the grass. But, and this was the only downside of the whole episode, it went all over the bottom of my robe—that I had let slip in the excitement of the jets flying overhead.

I shouted to Abu to keep his back to me. (My faithful bodyguard had not moved from his boulder despite the jets.) Crouching low, holding the back of my soiled robe well away from my bare legs, I staggered a few yards to the stream at the edge of the mountain saddle to wash the hemline of my robe in the fast-flowing water.

I was standing awkwardly on two boulders, reaching down between my legs, struggling to swirl the bottom of my stained robe around in the water, when the jets returned. I hadn't been expecting that. I looked up as they screamed overhead, wavered, put a hand out to balance myself, and fell backwards into the icy water. Abu ran up and helped me out of the stream without a word—even though I cursed him for watching me. We went back into the cave, and everyone was sensible enough not to ask why my robe was dripping wet.

I would have blamed the Americans if they had asked me. Mind you, for the first time ever, I was extremely grateful to the infidel. They had cleared my back passage most successfully. Allah be praised!

August 10.

Last month a Valerie Plame was outed by some journalist as a CIA operative. The interesting bit is that her husband is Joseph Wilson, the same Joseph Wilson, a former ambassador, who publicly disagreed with the White House claim that Iraq had obtained uranium from Niger, one of the main justifications for the war. Sounds like revenge to me. Anyway, I thought every man and his dog, not just me, knew who was a CIA operative and who wasn't, but it seems maybe not.

August 12

What can he offer her, that's what I want to know. What? I ask myself that question every day. The life he provides for her is so boring. Imagine living in the White House, surrounded by bureaucrats, never able to get out and follow her own interests. I cannot imagine it, however hard I try. Then think of the excitement and adventure she would enjoy if she were to join me. Laura is that type of woman, I am convinced of it; the adventurous kind, an individualist, a vital human being—like me.

I have a vision.

I see her striding across the Hindu Kush in her khaki fatigues and knee-high combat boots. The top of her shirt is unbuttoned, and drops of perspiration can be seen glistening on her glowing, suntanned breasts. A Kalashnikov is slung carelessly over one shoulder, a bandana of bullets is wound around her lithe body, and a band of devoted desperados follow behind her. Her short reddish hair bobs prettily beneath her beret (or does she wear a Rambo headband?) as her piercing turquoise eyes scan the horizon. She is the Che Guavara of Washington, a modern day Amazonian, the most feared female in al-Qaeda.

We would meet every few days, running in slow motion towards each other across the grass, arms outstretched, then grabbing a few moments of ecstasy in a cave or on a mountaintop. Discreetly, the others would withdraw—if we were in a cave. If we were on a mountaintop, we would be watched by unblinking goats—possibly *jealous* goats, thanks to Ali. Wherever we were, we would be in our own world. We would not care about any others. We would only have eyes for each other, two people of passion, of vision, of nobility.

She would tear frenziedly, greedily at my robe, while I stripped her combat shirt and trousers from her battle-scarred body.

"Is that a Colt 45 you have in your pocket," she would whisper breathlessly, nibbling my lips passionately, "or are you just pleased to see me?"

Our thirst for each other knows no bounds. Maybe we leave her boots on. I like those combat boots, and the way she digs them into my back as I ride her. We fall onto a mattress—or a bed of grass. My palm tree seeks out her oasis. Clasped together, whispering terms of endearment in each others ears—along with strategies for future battles and plots to overthrow her husband—I am driven to ever greater efforts to please her. The intensity of our love-making is the stuff of legend.

Thanks to me, she quickly forgets George and her once drunken, drug-crazed twins (easy enough to do, I imagine.) And she forgets her friends. She forgets everything, especially the meaningless existence she was once forced to suffer behind the doors of the White House. She even throws away her books, including her beloved Dostoevsky. I win her over. She dedicates her life to my cause. She becomes my strongest accomplice and most willing slave, as devoted to me as my men. Every day, she sends me off into battle satiated, scarcely able to stand upright, my back and shoulders scratched and bitten.

When she's not fighting, she's teaching the local children how to read. Sitting cross-legged on a dirt floor in an old hut high in the mountains, in her soft, low Texan accent she goes through the Dick & Jane series of early reading books. The peasants love her and press small gifts of food into her hands. In exchange, Laura insists on cleaning all their homes with Clorox.

She is brave enough to play such a part. She has a great soul. It is obvious to me. I can see it in her photographs. What is she doing with a waster like George, with a man whose policies she must despise? She is too good for him. She is letting her life pass her by. She is allowing him to suck the life force from her very core.

She must learn to see me for who I am.

August 21.

No reply from Downing Street to my email. That is so typical of Blair, believing in his own importance and ignoring the proffered hand of friendship.

August 30.

I've been thinking how, in1996, when the Taliban marched into Kabul, and Afghanistan became the first Muslim fundamentalist state in the modern world, one of their first actions was to ban television. They were so right to do so. This evil invention seduces the people towards the decadent way of life in the West. It corrupts all who view it, apart from strong-minded individuals like myself.

Under the Taliban, the penalty for possessing a television set was death by stoning. I congratulated Mullah Omar on the appropriateness of the punishment.

Of course, because no one was able to watch these public stonings on television (which I still believe, leaving aside the merits or otherwise of the medium, would have made an excellent educational program for pre-schoolers), the general populace was rounded up and told to make their way to the main square of whichever town it happened to be in, to watch the stoning live. On the whole, this was a most satisfactory arrangement, with the added advantage that the program was not interrupted by commercials.

I, myself did have television, and still do. Satellite TV. But as I said to Mullah Omar, when I met him for the first time on my return to Afghanistan from Sudan in 1996 to join the fight against the Russians: "It is necessary for me to have this evil western appliance in order that I may keep abreast of what is happening in the world, and especially in the land of Satan."

"Osama," he said, grasping my elbow in quite a familiar way as he did so (having donated so much money to the Taliban, I believe a certain degree of familiarity was excusable)—"Osama, I too must have a television for the very same reason. I hate it as much as you, and when I settle down before it in the evenings, instead of spending those hours in prayer as I would choose to do, I curse that box in the corner of my sitting room. Verily, I curse it. But if it means that we can continue to terrorize the West, then, for the sake of Allah, you and I must make such a sacrifice. We must watch that accursed, evil thing. It reveals much about our enemy."

We both nodded our heads and embraced each other sympathetically. I felt that Mullah Omar and I would definitely see eye to eye on most matters (even though he only has one eye), and that we would indeed be brothers.

I was tempted to ask him if he ever watched *The Simpsons,* which I happen to find extremely amusing and make a great effort to see every day, or *Neighbours.* This long-running Australian show has many merits, amongst which must be included the fact that it was the launch pad for the gorgeous Kylie and her *derrière.* However, I decided that it would be best to wait until I knew him better before asking such questions.

We were having tea together in the Great Hall of the People at the time, and all our advisers and hangers-on had been dismissed so that we could spend some time alone.

There was the sound of regular blows and groans from an adjoining room, but I thought it impolite to draw attention to these.

After a short pause I said: "I watch CNN and some BBC political programs."

"Ah yes," he replied. "You watch exactly the same as me. They are so boring, is it not so?"

"It is so," I said. "They are very boring programs. Terrible, biased propaganda, and quite mindless."

Someone cried out in agony from next door.

"Mind you," he continued, "they have many programs that are about you and I. Those are more interesting to watch. It pleases me greatly to see that they are so worried about the Taliban and also about your good self, and about our influence on the world stage."

"Most certainly we have them on the run," I agreed. "We are inside their heads, Mullah Omar, and they are deeply worried. They are like the sheep that finds itself caught between a wolf and a precipice. It does not know in which direction to turn."

There was a scuffling sound from next door, then several blows, followed by silence. I smiled awkwardly at my host.

He put a hand on my arm. "You must call me Om."

"Certainly. But in that case you must call me Os."

"Os and Om, that is a most satisfactory arrangement," and he smiled broadly, his one eye twinkling.

I continued: "I have video tapes of all the programs that have either mentioned my name or that of al-Qaeda. They are sent to me each month by a media-gathering organization in New York. As I'm sure you can imagine, Om, I now have a substantial library."

I thought I detected a flash of envy in his eyes before he replied: "I can imagine it would be so, Os. I too have a substantial library, but possibly it is not as well organized as yours. Too often I have been on the run, and have been forced to leave tapes behind. I am missing a great number. When I think about this, it quite upsets me."

We sipped our tea in silence. Next door I could now hear someone being flogged. It was too obvious to ignore. "Would you care to go next door and watch, Os?"

I declined. I find such events become a little tedious after awhile. If you've seen one flogging you've seen them all, that's what I always say.

"I would like to make it quite clear, Om, that I do not need these tapes in order that I may glorify my own image. That to me would be abhorrent, a sin against the will of Allah."

Mullah Omar nodded enthusiastically, saying over and over again, "Of course not, of course not! Heaven forbid. We two are but humble servants of Allah. Far be it for us..." But whatever he was about to say never materialized. He simply shrugged and smiled.

"I will sometimes allow my men to view these images on our television so that they may learn how greatly the West fears us. Not so often that there is any danger they will be corrupted, but perhaps every month or so. I like to show them— and they themselves love to see—the destruction of the World Trade Center in New York. They will cheer and clap their hands and insist that I play the tape again and again for their benefit. The tape is becoming quite worn out because of this, and I think I must soon replace it."

"You will be most happy with that success," he said.

I smiled humbly, nodding sagely, trying to look as if I was too modest to claim sole responsibility for such a great achievement (hiding my light under a Bush, as the President would say) but hoping nevertheless that he would apportion all of the success to me.

"The television, I find, is also the ideal instrument for illustrating to my men the stupidity of the President of the United States. Even when they see this fact for themselves on the television screen, they are sometimes unable to believe the imbecility of that man."

Mullah Omar let a small, rather high-pitched giggle escape from his beard, and nodded his head enthusiastically.

"These simple peasants will often turn on me," I continued, "and accuse me of playing tricks of them. 'You have digitally manipulated these images,' they will say, and it can sometimes take me a great deal of time to reassure them that the image has not been tampered with in any way, that what they see is what they get."

"Allah be praised for giving us such a foolish enemy. He is most munificent and compassionate to look after us in such a way."

I nodded wisely, being careful to portray my most statesmanlike air.

"Have you heard his most recent malapropism?" Omar asked, smiling broadly at me, thumping the arm of his chair with glee.

"Do tell me, Om. Which one is that? I hear so much about his mangling of the English language, I never know which is the latest."

"The President said: 'They misunderestimate me. I am a pitbull on the pant-leg of opportunity.'"

We both laughed so much at this malapropism, we had to clutch each other and almost fell off our cushions. Fortunately, there was no one around to see us. The truth is, I also wet myself a little I was laughing so much. I hoped it would not show up on my robe when I stood up.

"My favourite," I said, once I had recovered my breath, is: 'I know that the human being and the fish can coexist.'" This set us off again. We became quite hysterical for awhile. When we had finally recovered, I said:

"The question we must ask ourselves, Om, is this: is the man as stupid as he makes out, or is he so clever that he is fooling us all into thinking he is stupid?"

"No, no, no. Without any doubt whatsoever, he is as stupid as he seems."

"But there are those—I have seen their writings on the Net—who insist the President is not a moron after all—"

"Then they must be morons!" he shouted, and a flake of spittle hit me in the face.

I could see he was getting too excited; his one eye was blinking furiously. I said, "They insist that we are the stupid ones if we believe his idiocy is real."

"That I find hard to believe, Os. You are telling me that this man is so clever he has fooled us all these years? I find it most difficult to believe. He would have to be a very great actor to fool everyone into thinking he is an idiot when he is not. Remember that time when he said: 'It's clearly a budget. It's got a lot of numbers in it'? Could anyone make such a statement unless he is an out-and-out fool?"

I was forced to agree with my newfound friend. I have always tried very hard not to underestimate my enemy, but with a man like Bush it's easy enough to do.

If Blair was the American leader, I would be more wary. He, I believe, is a clever man. It is lucky he is only the leader of some pathetic little island stuck out in the middle of the North Sea where the people only have three subjects of interest: the weather, cricket and football.

Clinton was a clever man, too. They say he was one of the cleverest Presidents ever. I'm not sure what that says about the rest of them, but I am happy to believe that Clinton had an IQ a good deal higher than Bush's. Mind you, getting blow-jobs in the Oval Office when your wife—and not just any wife, but the formidable Hilary—is upstairs, that is not so intelligent. Perhaps his brain really is between his legs, as many people claim.

September 8.

Almost two years ago, Bush sat in some classroom for almost seven minutes staring at a kids' book, *The Pet Goat*. And it occurred to me: I think I've seen Ali reading that one, too.

September 20.

The best news I have heard for years. Some Israeli pilots have refused to attack targets in Palestine. As one can imagine, this has caused a bit of an uproar. Some of Israel's pilots have a conscience? Give over, I don't believe it. They'll probably be shot for that. I considered phoning Sharon and putting in a word on their behalf, but then decided this could well make matters worse for the pilots, so resisted the temptation. Anyway, I do so hate speaking to the man: he tries to be funny, but it's in a slow, ponderous, boring way, his jokes like some lumbering Soviet Antonov AN225 that can barely lift off the runway.

September 22.

The Neiman-Marcus Christmas catalogue arrived today. This morning I spent a happy hour leafing through it. Most annoyingly, the messenger was ambushed by the Americans somewhere, and there is a bullet hole right through the middle of the catalogue. The messenger was killed, but happily the Yanks never bothered to confiscate the catalogue. I don't know what the store will make of the bullet hole when I send in my order.

Have already decided to buy mainly for myself this year, although I will buy each of the wives a little something—maybe Armani, Ferragamo, Prado or Donna Karan. Can't make up my mind if I should also get a small gift for Samah. It may make her look more favorably on me again, although I have no wish to upset Mohammed. And have made up my mind to buy Abu some Gucci Pour

Homme aftershave—although that is really for my own benefit, to try and stifle some of his natural odors.

September 24.

I've been remembering the time when I was studying in Beirut, when I was about 17.

I was shocked when I first saw the women's legs so flagrantly exposed, and the way they wore make up and left their faces uncovered. That's the very first thing I noticed when I arrived in the Country. I quickly realized how sheltered my background had been.

For about a year I kept to the straight and narrow, averting my gaze from all temptations and keeping my head buried in my books. It was only when a group of businessmen from back home took me to the Pink Pussycat nightclub that my eyes were opened. That was when I went off the rails big time.

The Pink Pussycat, Adam and Eve's and the Kasbah, those were my favorite nightclubs. And I received privileged service in all of them. I splashed the money around in those days, and it bought me everything I wanted: the best tables, the most beautiful women, the most expensive champagne, and the most convivial companions. Every night it was the same story.

Sometimes I woke up in the morning and was unable to remember what had happened the night before. Most mornings I would see, through bleary, half closed eyes, a woman (sometimes two) lying beside me in bed, and she might conjure up some vague recollection of what had happened the evening before. But often she wouldn't.

It was the women in the Pink Pussycat whom I shall never forget. Never will I be able to erase them from my memory. Especially Sabrina, the English blonde. She was expensive but, Allah be praised, she knew how to give pleasure to a man. She had so many appliances in her bedroom, there was scarcely any room left for the bed. And she introduced me to all of them.

I was hesitant at first, but gradually she persuaded me of the exquisite pleasure—and pain!—they could arouse. The hours I spent strapped in those appliances, or to the bed, passed in a blur, every sense of my body satiated—and many times over. I don't wish to boast, but I was still in my teens then and could come five, six or seven times a night. Often I would not fall asleep until the first call to prayer.

That woman had a yoni to die for, and gladly would I have passed away with her straddling me, pounding up and down on my rigid member, her breasts brushing against my youthful, upturned eager face.

Although I paid her well for her company, I believe she had a soft spot for me: I like to think I was her favorite customer. She told me many times that she loved me, but then I am not an idiot. I could also see the way her face lit up when I took out my wallet in the mornings.

We also met away from the Pink Pussycat. It was our secret. I would pick her up from her apartment in my Mercedes (a car I loved even more than Sarah) and we'd drive up into the mountains for the day. We'd take a picnic with us (how immodest I was in those days: caviar, champagne, canapés, strawberries and other such delicacies were our usual fare), and we'd lie beside a river, eat, then make love on the rug. Afterwards we'd bathe together in the river. I am still able to see her body glistening in the water, her long blonde hair spread out around her in the rushing waters.

Her hair would spread out like that, in exactly the same way, when the roof was down in the Mercedes. She would shout, sing and laugh as I drove. Once she gave me a blow job at over one hundred miles an hour. How I never crashed that car, I do not know. I was drunk often enough when I drove it, and remember hitting the curb with some frequency. I scraped another car once, and had to get the whole of one side of the car panel beaten. The other car's owner never discovered who had hit him, so I never had to pay for his repairs, which was a piece of good fortune.

Much of the time I was chauffeur driven. The chauffeur was some obsequious local, and the way he kowtowed to me all the time gave me the creeps. I think my family found him somewhere, and therefore he felt particularly obligated to them to make sure that no harm came to me. He was certainly over-protective, and if I wanted the car by myself, to go off with Sabrina or one of the other girls, I would have to achieve this through trickery and deception. He was hard work, that man, and quite without any sense of humor.

I would have been content to live in Beirut for the rest of my life, but then the war started. The Christians were to blame, they are always to blame. My ultra-conservative family, who always like to have something to worry about, demanded that I immediately return to Jiddah, for my own safety. I protested, but they insisted.

I almost took Sabrina back with me (imagine the storm of outrage if I had done so), but then, thinking that I would only be away for a few weeks, I left her behind.

"I'll be back soon," I promised her on our last night together, "as soon as this trouble blows over." But I was never to see her again. The trouble never did blow over, and is still raging thirty years on.

Once I was back in Jiddah, and realized I was going to be there longer than a few weeks, I bought another car: this time a red Mercedes SL 450. That was some car. Once I got it up to almost one hundred and fifty miles an hour out in the desert. It flew.

A cop stopped me one evening, and would have given me a ticket, but when I told him who my Dad was, and how he was friendly with the Royal Family and everything—I just casually dropped that into the conversation!—he let me go with a caution. The fact I also slipped several hundred riyal into his hand may have helped.

Women fell for the car big time. Some of them almost came just sitting in the front seat. They are so predictable, women.

Of course my family disapproved of my lifestyle, but couldn't do much about it. I would get these lectures from my uncles and older brothers, but I ignored them. I despised them all. I was determined to have a good time, to continue the kind of life I had begun to enjoy in Beirut. I wasn't interested in the construction world, and found business really boring. It might have been how my family made their money, but it still didn't interest me.

No matter how discreet I tried to be (drinking out in the desert, taking women back to the flats of friends, and generally not going out of my way to publicize my comings and goings), people soon started talking. My family always seemed to hear about what I had been up to. Everything reached their ears eventually, and they were only too ready to believe the worst they heard about me.

I was barely talking to any of them when, finally, Salim saved my life. "Younger brother," he said to me over the phone one evening, "join me in the Hajj(3)."

For some reason, even though I wasn't particularly close to him, barely knew him in fact, I agreed to accompany him. I had to make the pilgrimage at least once in my life, so why not now? Why not get it over with? That was the way I reasoned then, and I believe he did too. Neither of us was that enthusiastic about going.

I'm still not sure what happened to me on the Hajj, but it changed my life. Overnight I became a new person, a different person, and for that I shall always be grateful to my oldest brother—may he rest in peace with Allah. He it was who set me on the right path.

From being a person who barely thought about Allah and rarely prayed the required five times a day, I overnight became a devout convert. I found God. He transformed my life. From then on I devoted myself to Him body and soul.

On returning to Jiddah, I sold my Mercedes, dropped all of those friends who refused to give up alcohol and their immoral ways (ninety-nine per cent of them), and no longer had anything to do with loose women. Instead, I went regularly to the mosque, and prayed five times a day—at least. And my family welcomed me back with open arms. The hypocrites.

So maybe it was a good thing that I went to Beirut. Perhaps I had to wander from the right path in order to find it again.

September 30.

The Justice Department has launched a full scale enquiry into the leak about Joseph Wilson's wife being in the CIA. Wilson is pointing the finger at Rove and the White House, both of whom (surprise, surprise) are denying, with looks of wide-eyed innocence, any involvement. It sounds like a Rove tactic: cast aspersions. It doesn't matter if they're true, or even plausible, as long as people talk about them and ask questions, some mud will stick.

I'm not sure why Wilson is wasting his time—because wasting his time, he is. That Machiavellian Himmler look-alike will be too wily for him.

October 4.

That Rafiq is a pig. That is how he eats: like a pig. His mouth performs some weird circular motion, and while it does so, masticating the food for an inordinately long period of time, he keeps it open so that we may all enjoy the sight. It is like staring into a cement mixer. No one else seems to notice. Often he sits opposite me, however hard I try to avoid such a position, and it is impossible for me not to see. He will make matters worse, either by recounting some tale or other as he eats, or by sticking a hand into his mouth—which sometimes looks as if it is about to disappear completely—again while he eats, and foraging around for a bone or a piece of gristle or whatever it is that is bothering him.

I can't bear the man.

October 9.

Condoleezza Rice. Now there's a name to conjure with. And, unlike Laura, she's available. Why's she available, I wonder? Why has she not been swept off her feet by someone? She's OK looking, and I imagine she's worth a bit. (They call her Bush's "poorest millionaire" and say that a Chevron oil tanker has been named after her—modest enough beginnings.) Maybe her heart belongs to Daddy? She's certainly never out of his company.

She's a bit frightening in a strange kind of way, but she'd be easier to seduce than Laura.

Certainly worth considering….

Of course, there's always the Silver Fox. Wow! Now she really is frightening. Tricky Dicky called her a woman who knows how to hate—praise indeed from Mr. Hate himself. Maybe she'd be good for me: absolutely no fear of her ever becoming over-emotional. Only problem is, I'm not into grannies.

It's interesting how the Bush men are so weak (well, George and his Dad in particular), and they surround themselves with really tough women: Laura, Barbara, Rice and Karen Hughes to name just four off the top of my head. Tough cookies all of them. Ball breakers certainly, possibly even man haters, but I could cope with Laura: she just needs a man, and then I'm sure she'd be as sweet as "Mom's homemade apple pie."

October 12.

A delivery of Michael's Frozen Custard from Madison, Wisconsin. Got Caramel Cashew, Butter Pecan, Death by Chocolate and, of course, the favorite for us purists, the Vanilla. I order them online and they're delivered to an address in Kandahar, then transported as quickly as possible to wherever I am at the time.

(For a name on the order form I use the clever little anagram, bin Noselad, that I don't think they will be quick to crack.)

Michael's Custard is famous for being made fresh every two hours. By the time they reach me they've been around longer than is ideal, but the cold mountain air helps to keep them in pretty good condition.

I make sure none of the others see them. I don't like to share.

October 16,

Already it seems that winter is here. We huddle in the caves, wrapped in every piece of clothing we own, and think of those down in the valleys who are dry and warm. Sometimes my teeth chatter so hard I think they will fall out. If we light a fire—safe enough to do at night in a cave—we're definitely warmer, but it means that in some of the smaller caves we are scarcely able to breathe.

The mornings are hell—if hell can be this cold. I always pretend to be asleep, buried in my sleeping bag with only the tip of my nose exposed. I wait patiently, half awake and half asleep, until someone else gets up and either lights the fire or brews some tea. Sometimes I am brought a glass of tea in bed, and that can be like the highlight of my day. Bliss! I think that is reasonable enough: one of the perks of being the boss.

Abu doesn't seem to feel the cold, but my guess is that this is because he is covered by a good, thick layer of fat.

October 22.

The NATO commander in Afghanistan says that his men are increasingly facing "excellently trained" terrorists. Praise indeed! Mullah Omar and I congratulate each other. We obviously have the enemy worried.

October 29.

Release another video to Arabic TV taunting Bushy. Think it will really annoy him. Certainly hope so!

November 1.

Forcing the Russians out of Afghanistan was one of the highpoints of my career. What a great victory that was. We took on one of the world's two superpowers, and we beat them. They didn't know what hit them. It was just like David fighting Goliath. I shall go down in history for that feat alone: my immortality is assured.

More to the point, I feel it atoned, to a great extent, for my sinful past. I told people that one day's participation in the jihad in Afghanistan was the equivalent of a thousand days of praying in an ordinary mosque. That should stand me in good stead one day.

Once I was only twenty yards from the Russians. They were trying to capture me. They had heard so much about my deeds—I was famous even as far away as Moscow—that they could not wait to get their hands on me.

I was under heavy bombardment, but I was so peaceful in my heart that I fell asleep. Yes, Allah be praised, it is true. I fell fast asleep. I slept the sleep of innocence. This experience has been written about in Islam's earliest books.

I saw a 120mm mortar shell land right in front of me, but it did not blow up. Four more bombs were dropped from a Russian plane onto our headquarters but they did not explode either.

I beat the Soviet Union. The Russian army fled in disarray. It was truly a great victory for me.

I have never been afraid of death. As a Muslim, I believe that when I die I shall go to heaven. And before every battle, God sends me tranquility. So I am at peace when I go to war.

Everyone I fought with in Afghanistan was pleased with me, and not just because I gave them my money. Over the years I have given them more than $100 million—American dollars. But it was much more than that. It was because I left my palaces to go and live among the peasants and the fighters. I cooked my food with them, and I ate with them, and I dug trenches alongside them. And all of that impressed them mightily.

The truth is, they are easily impressed.

But they preferred me to those Mujahideen leaders who roared around the countryside in their jeeps, always shouting orders at everyone, but never going anywhere near the fighting. The only time those leaders appeared was when there was a television news team in the area. They were attracted to the cameras like bees to honey.

It was little wonder the ordinary Afghanistan fighters loved me. They would have followed me anywhere. And that is still true today. If Bush wonders why he cannot capture me now, it is because I am surrounded by so many friends. These people, they will lay down their lives before they allow me to be taken. The American cowboy does not understand that.

They are a very loyal people, the Afghans. It is also the fact that they are very stupid.

It is true the Country sank into chaos after our great victory, after we had thrown out the Russians, but that was not my fault. Maybe I should have stayed there so that order could be restored. But everyone was fighting everyone, all the greedy warlords wanted to line their own pockets, and no one was interested in thinking about the bigger picture.

How selfish and greedy these people are, these ordinary mortals. Am I the only person who is capable of seeing beyond the end of my nose?

November 5.

Had a brilliant idea today. Sometimes I amaze even myself.

I thought that for our next video we should get some existing footage of the House of Representatives in Washington, or the Houses of Parliament in London, or somewhere like that, and then, using all the computer wizardry that's available nowadays, have me sitting on a park bench or on the steps outside.

Imagine, me right in the very heart of Washington or London, with people walking past, feeding the pigeons, eating their sandwiches or whatever it is these people do, and the scourge of the West is addressing the world from right amongst them. Think of the uproar.

I imagine the CIA or MI5 saying to each other, "How did he do it? It's not possible that he delivered one of his speeches right in our midst. How did he slip across our borders?"

Of course, Ayman put a damper on it immediately. "They'll know it's just special effects. They'll spot it immediately."

"It doesn't matter. Who cares! It's the symbolism, don't you get it? Think how upset they'll be."

"Osama, if we could do it for real, it would be a great idea. But we can't do it for real, so forget it."

He is such a spoilsport, that man. At times I don't think he can see beyond procuring his next little boy.

November 9.

We are bored. All we could think to do this evening was play Monopoly again—with the board I bought years ago when I lived in London. (I just love these capitalist games from the West!) To be honest, I'm sometimes not sure why I put myself through this, as Ayman always wins. I'm convinced he cheats, but he's so good at cheating no one ever catches him out.

It was the usual story this evening, so when I realized my deputy was going to win, I told everyone I was tired and wanted to go to bed. I couldn't face seeing that smug grin of his any longer, and the way he preens himself. He sits there on his cushion, stroking his beard like some domestic cat grooming itself, while he surveys his property empire, his little rows of houses and hotels. I'm sure he was a slum landlord in a previous life, probably in New York.

He pretends he doesn't care that he's winning, but it's so obvious he does. It's this pretence that makes me mad.

The rot set in when he landed on Mayfair. As Omar already had Park Lane, I didn't think there was anything to worry about. How naive of me!

After about fifteen minutes of nagging and whispering in his ear, Ayman persuaded Omar to swap Park Lane for three Stations. I couldn't believe it. The man is an idiot. Park Lane for three Stations, when the recipient already has Mayfair, how stupid is that.

I said, "Don't do it, Omar, don't do it."

He grinned at me in that sweet, *dumb* way of his, and said: "But I already have one Station, Osama, so now I'll have four."

Some people have no strategic sense, none at all. Either that, or Ayman has some kind of hold over Omar. I sometimes think that is a distinct possibility. His face is certainly babyish enough to appeal to my deputy.

Of course, Ayman immediately put hotels on Mayfair and Park Lane and, as he already had hotels on Bond Street, Regent Street and Oxford Street, that side of the board was now a complete no-go area.

The first time I went round there, after he had put hotels on Park Lane and Mayfair, I landed on Liverpool Street Station. Omar wasn't paying attention; he was cleaning his rifle. I've told him not to do that when we're playing Monopoly because he gets oil all over the dice, but he lives in his own world and doesn't even listen to me. Anyway, I got off scot-free.

He noticed where I'd landed when my next turn came round, but I had already thrown the dice. He still tried to make me pay, but I refused.

"He's thrown the dice, camel dung! You're too late," shouted Abu on my behalf. Omar was really upset, and blushed furiously, even though we were only talking a £200 fine. He takes the game far too seriously.

On my following throw, I picked up a Community Chest card and went directly to Jail. That was a relief. I had the option of paying a fine or going to Jail, but I felt much safer in Jail with all those hotels and houses on the board. And the longer I stayed there the better.

I only had houses on Euston Road, Angel Islington and Pentonville Road, but the amount of money I made when someone landed on one of those was barely worth the trouble of collecting. Ayman was unnecessarily rude when he landed on one of my properties earlier in the game, volunteering to pay even before I had shouted "Rent!" That may sound like he was being kind, volunteering like that, but he wasn't, far from it. He did it in that really smarmy way of his, a nasty way.

"How much is it, Osama? £250 or something?" he sneered.

Sometimes if he didn't have the right money, he'd throw £100 across the board for a £75 rent payment for example and say, in a horribly condescending way, "Keep the change." I could have been a waiter in a rundown Cairo restaurant the way he addressed me. I don't think it's a very nice way to behave.

So I decided to stay in Jail as long as possible. Sadly, it wasn't long enough. Just when you don't want to throw a double, that's exactly what you do. I had to leave Jail! I didn't want the others to see how reluctant I was to move out, so I said, "Oh good, two sixes!" in a loud voice. Being the boss, you can't afford to show fear at times like that. When the chips are down, you have to stand up and be counted. That's part of being a leader. About three shakes of the dice later, I landed on Mayfair. I sometimes think Allah has it in for me.

"That'll be rent, Osama," Ayman said in his creepiest voice.

He had this smug, self-congratulatory grin on his chubby face, and his eyes were lit up behind his spectacles. I almost expected to see pound signs in there, like on poker machines when you hit the jackpot.

"That will be two thousand big ones, my old friend."

I wanted to gag when I heard that "my old friend." Instead I shrugged, trying to look indifferent as I half handed, half threw, the money across the board to him.

"Well, that's me just about out of the game now," I said as casually as I could. "Not that I care," I added, "I'm feeling pretty tired, and was thinking of retiring anyway. I'll leave you four to it."

"Oh come on, Os," they all shouted. "Don't be such a spoilsport."

"I'm not being a spoilsport. I'm tired, that's all. Don't pick on me."

"But we haven't finished the game yet."

"Well, I wasn't going to win, that's for sure, and I'm tired. Can't a man go to bed when he's tired?"

There was much moaning and tutting, but I ignored them all and came to bed. Now I must stop writing. I want to try and be asleep before Abu comes to bed. I take two sleeping pills to help me on my way. I still wake up half way through the night. I light a candle and try to get off to sleep again by reading the book that is always at my bedside, *Stupid White Men*.

November 21.

"Oh Allah, save me from this filth! Oh, if you could but see what I can see, you would not believe your eyes. And if you did believe your eyes, then you would tear them out and cast them as far from you as possible. Oh, but this is the very depths of depravity and iniquity. Allah, protect me from such evil!"

These are the kinds of thing I say in a loud voice when I am browsing porn sites on the web. They are for the benefit of my brothers-in-arms who are sitting close to me, but on the other side of the flimsy partition that is used to separate my office from the rest of the command center.

No one is allowed into my office when I am sending or receiving messages from our units around the world. To my more intellectually challenged disciples I explain this by means of a little homily. I tell them that al-Qaeda is like a bunch of grapes. We are all on the same vine, and yet we are all separate and independent. If one grape should be plucked from the vine, it will be unable to tell its interrogators—those who *tread* it, that is a little joke I always insert at this point—anything about the other grapes on the vine. By keeping our people separate and independent, we shall remain impenetrable to the outside world, to the infidel. Secrecy, I emphasize, is all important.

"Know only what you have to know, and no more," I say in conclusion. Usually, at this point, they stare at me blankly.

It is generally known by now that al-Qaeda communicates through encrypted messages on internet porn sites. Even those idiot Americans have discovered this. But being aware of this simple fact has not made it any easier for them to break our codes. The porn sites are so vast and change so rapidly, and our codes so sophisticated that for the FBI or CIA or—what do those fools call it now? National Homeland Security or something—it is like looking for one particular grain of sand in the Sahara. Only harder.

And talking about harder, every time I go onto these sites to send or retrieve messages, that is exactly what I become.

I still remember when I went to the Lebanon as a seventeen year old and saw women's legs for the very first time, the shock it gave me! Sometimes when they sat down, I would see their knees, even some of their thighs—a sight that would almost cause me to pass out. But what can be seen on the internet, well, it makes what I saw as a seventeen year old look like an alim's(4) tea party. It almost beggars description. My hand shakes so much just thinking about it, I find it difficult to write.

Sometimes when I am studying these sites, I am tempted to shout to my colleagues to come and have a look too. I want to share with someone else these unbelievable visions that are on my screen. I want someone to confirm that they really are there, that I have not been holed up in the Hindu Kush for so long that my brain has become affected, that I am suffering from hallucinations.

However, I appreciate this would scarcely be a wise move, so instead—sometimes even when I am tugging furiously at the palm tree—I will cry out: "Oh infamy! Oh horrors! Oh depravity in the name of progress! Oh, oh, oh…" I do not think they suspect anything.

I have seen breasts the size of giant melons, and every other size too. Even breasts that are like walnuts on the chest of a pre-pubescent girl. And pudenda…Shameful, blatant, one-eyed monsters like that of Mullah Omar himself. They, too, come in every size, every shape and every color. Often the harlot is parting her lips with her hands as if she is drawing back the curtains and inviting one in. "Would you like to peak inside my temple?" It is an invitation that would tempt the devil himself.

Some of these parts have great unshaven bushes, wild bushes (like the President himself—ha, ha!), while some have what I believe are called "bikini cuts." These bikini cut bushes remind me of the head of a Mohawk Indian.

And many of these sacred sites are shaved to look as bald as the day their owners were born. I am not quite sure what to make of such pudenda. They look too naked to me, too obscene. Personally, I think that a covering of hair, trimmed or otherwise, is more natural and makes what is not, let's face it, at the end of the day, so fine a sight, a good deal more attractive. Hair teases more; it is like the veil over the female face, it stimulates the imagination.

But still, each pudendum is interesting in itself, without any doubt at all that much is true. It takes all sorts, is that not what they say? If every oasis was exactly the same, how boring would that be. When a man is thirsty, he likes to quench his thirst at different watering holes.

What I find most interesting when I carry out my research on the internet is that all of these genitalia are in close up, as if their owners are determined the viewer should miss nothing. These private parts are practically falling out of the screen, and are virtually in your face. It is most astonishing.

There are men there, too, usually "doing it" to a woman. Yes, it is possible to see that, too: the man sticking his thing into a woman's thing. Is nothing in America sacred, I wonder?

It does affect me nevertheless, I would be the first to admit that. I am most ashamed of the affect such sights have on me, but I most truly believe that there is not a red-blooded male this side of the Sahara desert who could remain unaffected.

Even when the man is perverse and is sticking his thing into the wrong orifice, I am affected. Or it can be two men in different orifices—as well as the mouth. I have seen a woman penetrated from every direction at the same time, every orifice I can imagine, and some I did not even know about. They make her look like something that is ready to be put on the barbecue, skewered right through.

Often these men are black. I think, after having seriously studied the internet for awhile, that Americans have an inferiority complex—white Americans that is. They like to look at black men because they are so well-endowed. Some of them, it is true, are massive, some of them even make me feel inferior. Their palm tree can look like the arm of a baby. But I am not fixated, as some Americans most assuredly are, by the size of the black man's palm tree—and his coconuts too, that sometimes look like they are too heavy to hang in place and are about to fall onto the bed, or the floor, or wherever.

I have also seen—and this I am not so happy about—men together. This I am not so keen on. I think it is necessary to draw the line somewhere. The truth is, if I had my way, I would stone these men. They are doing what a man and a woman do together, everything that a man and a woman do together, but it is between men. And I think I shall leave it at that. It isn't necessary to embellish the matter any further, except to say that it is worse than doing it to a camel.

I would not look at these sites myself, but there is an al-Qaeda sleeper in Sydney, and another one in San Francisco, who always send their messages on these sites which show men. So, of course, it is necessary for me to look at them. It cannot be avoided.

I wonder if these two sleepers are that way inclined. It would seem so. If this is true, then I am displeased. I do not think that I want people like that in al-Qaeda. How can a man fight for Allah when he is sticking his palm tree into black sand, or an oil well?

Sometimes it can be quite frenetic when I am on these sites. I am trying to send messages while I am receiving other messages. I am shouting out things like, "Oh, this is filthy, this is vile! Oh Allah, save me from drowning in this sewage!" for the benefit of those next door. And there are porn pop-ups, introductions to new sites, coming up on the screen faster than I can close them down. They seem to have a life of their own. As soon as I click on the "X" in the top right hand corner of one site, three more will pop up on my screen. It is like Hercules and the Gorgon: cut off one site and many others grow in its place.

As often as not, while all of this is going on, amongst this visual bedlam, I am attempting to pull myself off. I say "attempting" because it can be quite distracting to have all this happening on the screen at the same time, and to have one hand clicking away frantically on the mouse while the other is tugging away furiously at the palm tree. It is every bit as tricky as patting one's head with one hand while rubbing one's stomach with the other. When I was a child, I was never any good at that, either.

One of my pet hates about these porn sites is the unceasing demand for my credit card details. When al-Qaeda first started using these sites for encrypted messages, I never gave out my credit card details, no matter how tempting the sites were.

But it could sometimes become very annoying, not to say frustrating. Messages would pop up on the screen like, "As much pussy as you want, absolutely free," "Free porn!" another one would say, and "The hottest babes in the world, no charge!" from another.

So naturally enough, I think, Ah good, free porn—as indeed would anyone. But no sooner do I click on one of these sites than up comes a message: "Fill in your credit card details below, along with your email address, then you can enjoy free membership of this site for a month. After one month, we will charge you." What a rort! That is nothing less than misleading advertising. Such practices should be stamped out. Only in America could a person get away with such a confidence trick.

I stuck it out for awhile, but eventually I succumbed. It was too tempting. I would see a ravishingly beautiful woman lying on her back, her legs spread wide enough to take a camel, and she'd be staring at me with this blatant, cute, come hither smile, obviously saying something along the lines of, "C'mon big boy. Wanna give it to me? I'd like that. Sock it to me, sexy. Just give me your credit card details…"

And covering her most treasured possession would either be a dirty great big red cross or a smudge. The latter would be like trying to peer through a steamy mirror. You couldn't see anything at all, at least not the bit you wanted to see, until you'd parted with your credit card details. The most important bit was out of focus, as if it had been filmed by Mohammed.

You could see her face all right, but let's be honest, that was the bit you weren't in the slightest bit interested in seeing. They could put a donkey's head on those shoulders, and nobody would give a damn. To hell with her face, put a burka over it for all I care. Let's see her pussy.

Sometimes there'd even be a man straddling her (supposed to represent the viewer in all probability. Like, put yourself here, in his shoes—even though he wasn't wearing any), and this man's thing has disappeared behind the big red cross too, or been smudged out as well. And that can be frustrating, even though it's only a man's thing. I mean, you know what's going on behind the big red cross and the dirty great smudge, but you still want to see it for yourself. You just want to make sure it's exactly how you imagine, that they haven't somehow managed to come up with something new.

So I succumbed; I would hand over my credit card details. And I have to say, I've never regretted doing so. It has been a real education. All the big red crosses and smudges have gone out of my life for good. Everything is now in focus, nothing is blocked out.

I have so many credit cards, and I have used them all many times over. I joined so many porn sites I eventually got a query from Abu-al-Hasan, al-Qaeda's main accountant, our financial whiz kid and money man. He emailed me: "Hey, Os, watcha doing joining all them pussy sites?"

Boy, I thought, this guy knows everything. So I emailed him back that it was essential I was a member of these sites—or that al-Qaeda was ("nothing to do with me personally," I reassured him, "they're not my cup of tea at all")—because no matter how they offended me, no matter how nauseous I became when I logged onto them, no matter how repulsed I was by the decadent imagery to be seen there, it was the perfect way for our brothers-in-arms to communicate. He has never queried the use of my credit cards since.

Of course, most of my credit cards are in the names of charities al-Qaeda uses as a cover. I sometimes wonder what the banks think about the Sudanese Welfare Society or the Afghan Veterans Support Group, for instance, running up enormous bills at Hot and Wet, or Pussy Galore, or Teenage Vampire Virgins.

There was a time when I logged onto adult chat shows, too, just for fun. I always logged on as George and, when pressed, told people that yes, I was President of the United States of America. It was always good for a laugh.

A few of the women I met on these sites were really a bit wild. They'd take you into what are called private chat rooms and they'd do things to you, and let you do things to them that still make me blush. But it was only done in cyber space, of course, in one's imagination. Still, it could be quite stress relieving nevertheless.

What put me off at the end of the day was when I heard that on these sites not only do people frequently lie about their ages, their marital status, their employment, where they lived and just about everything else in their lives—none of which bothered me in the least (how could it when I was going around saying I was the President of the United States), but they often lied about their sex, too.

That did worry me. That worried me enormously. I said to myself, what if some woman's getting you all steamed up in one of those private rooms, and you're tugging away furiously because of all the nice things she's saying to you, then she sends through a message saying that *she* is in fact a ninety year old *widower?*

I think that would really mess with your head. So I gave it away.

November 22.

I am persecuted. I really feel that. They are persecuting me, hounding me, hunting me like an animal, making my life a misery. It is most unfair. I do not deserve to be picked on in such a way. The whole world treats me like a leper.

Helicopters fly overhead all day and all night. Marines and Special Service Forces are skulking over every horizon. They bomb my caves—my homes—incessantly. They cross-examine the locals every day, and promise bigger, more tempting rewards for my capture—or death. They are offering to pay people a fortune to kill me, imagine that! They are making my life *unlivable*!!

I hate them. I hate their arrogance and their power and the way they think the world belongs to them. They are so self-righteous! I hate that too. I wish they would leave me in peace. I want to stop running. I want to rest. I don't want to spend the rest of my life looking over my shoulder, never knowing who I can trust, never having an opportunity to catch my breath. I want to be left alone. I want to stop stuffing myself with Valium.

I have this dream. I am lying in a hammock, strung between two palm trees (real palm trees), in an oasis. My wives are around me, feeding me tidbits and letting me sip from a goblet of wine. There is music playing, birds are singing, and I am drowsy. I can hear the trickle of water nearby. But—and this is the essence of the dream—I am totally relaxed, totally at ease. I do not have a worry in the world—apart from deciding which of the ladies I shall service next.

Laura is in a nearby hut preparing dinner.

November 23.

I do not know what came over me yesterday. I was feeling a little down, that is all. I was allowing them to get to me. It was a depression caused by this atrocious weather, that is all. I took some Valium and had a few nips of whisky, and today I'm back on my feet again.

Hemorrhoids return. It must be our lousy diet.

November 25.

We are in the mountains to the north west of the main Kabul-Kandahar road. It is a desolate region, and relatively low compared to the mountains along the Afghanistan-Pakistan border: around 10,000 feet on average. Not being so high up makes the weather slightly more bearable at this time of year. There are few roads and only two or three small villages: Tarin Kowt, Zin and Kandu-Ye Bala. The locals know us and are happy to let us sleep in their homes. The facilities are basic—often more basic than in our command centers—but the warmth of their hospitality more than makes up for this.

November 28.

Bush has visited Iraq in top secrecy and celebrated Thanksgiving with American troops. I have to admit he has achieved a public relations coup. (Must have been Rove's idea in that case.) But it has also given me an idea: why don't I turn the tables on him and go to New York? I could perform *salat*(5) with fellow Muslims, and we could distribute *zakat*(6) together.

Imagine…Actually, I can't. But I shall hand the task over to Ayman, and let him think of a way to achieve this.

By the time I'm back in my cave in Afghanistan, the Americans will be opening their morning newspapers to read how I unrolled my *sajjada*(7) for midday prayer on a Friday in New York's Central Mosque.

December 1.

Abu Bakar Bashir's conviction has been overturned in Indonesia, because they were unable to prove he was the leader of the Islamic militant group, Jemaah Islamiah. Good news: they won't make him into a martyr now. I don't need the competition.

That man worries me. He really does look holy, like one of those saints dreamed up by the Vatican, bleeding from all his stigmata while he feeds little birds and blesses children. He even has twinkling eyes, like some kindly old granddad. I certainly feel I'm losing out to him in the "let's look saintly" stakes.

He is always smiling. It's quite sickening. I can't compete. Even when they're dragging him into court, he's smiling. He gives the impression he wouldn't hurt a fly, but from what I hear, he'd be more than happy to blow up his own granny. As they always say, there's no smoke without fire.

I must study him, try and discover how he manages to fool everyone so successfully.

December 2:

How can Laura live in a house with such a bunch of illiterates? She's always trying to teach poor people how to read and write, but maybe she should start with those in the US Government.

The annual "Foot in Mouth Prize" awarded by the UK's Plain English campaign has been awarded to Rumsfeld for his: "Reports that say that something hasn't happened are always interesting to me, because as we know, there are known knowns; there are things we know we know. We also know there are known unknowns; that is to say we know there are some things we do not know. But there are also unknown unknowns—the ones we don't know we don't know." That is a gem.

Arnold Schwarzenegger was one of the runners-up (I didn't even know he could speak—I thought he simply grunted as he swung through the trees, beating his chest.) Say no more.

Except to say, I think there must be a competition on in the White House. I bet Bush, Rumsfeld, Cheney et al get together at the weekend and award a prize to whichever one of them has made the most gibberish, nonsensical comment during the week, and got away with it. Surely such comments must be intentional? I bet they have a good laugh.

December 13.

The infidels have captured that overrated dictator, Hussein. (Go to Jail, go directly to Jail, do not pass Go, do not collect £200.)

They have dragged him from a hole in the ground like the dirty, stinking, unshaven rat that he is. He was disheveled. He looked like a tramp off the streets of New York. What an ignominious end, to be seen on the television screens of the world in that condition, unkempt and unwashed. Some doctor was even seen inspecting his scalp for lice (but they did not say whether or not they found any, which was disappointing. I'm sure they must have done.)

I will not end up like that. Abu, and all of my followers, have strict instructions that, should we be surrounded and there is absolutely no way out, than they must shoot me. They have all sworn to do so. That is a martyr's end, far better than to be left rotting in some American jail or at the mercy of some trumped up international kangaroo court.

I am surprised Saddam has survived so long.

The man is an idiot. He is a crook and a dictator. He is an erector of grandiose statues of himself, a torturer of soccer players and political opponents. He is a common thief and a liar. He is a builder of appalling taste, his palaces a frightening mix of kitsch and gold leaf. He is a coward. He is a conniving, two-faced, sexual profligate. He is a deviant. He is greedy. He is a disgrace to Islam and a mean, nasty womanizer. He is vain, arrogant, pompous and stupid—really stupid. He is a blasphemer. In short, I am not too fond of the man.

I never had any time for him. He pretends to be a Muslim, but he is not. He worships only himself and his gross family. The only sad thing about his demise is that the Americans are in his country, and do not look as if they are keen to leave. (I can hear them siphoning off the oil as I write this.)

But, if the truth be told, it is good news that the Americans have invaded the Country because it has given al-Qaeda a wonderful opportunity. My men are in there now, with more joining every day, to fight the Americans. We will make it so unpleasant for them, they will eventually leave.

My dream is that the allies will fight amongst themselves (as France and the US are already doing), the governments of Saudi Arabia and Pakistan will collapse, and we can then turn our attention to the pro-Western Islamic governments like Egypt and Yemen. Finally, I shall end up as caliph of a unified, Middle Eastern caliphate.

I have my dreams. And, thanks to Bush, they are slowly becoming reality. Without his help I do not know that they would be possible. Everything would certainly be much harder to achieve.

The only fly in the ointment is this: will America ever desert Saudi Arabia? I cannot imagine any US President having to tell his people that the days of cheap oil have gone forever. My task is therefore to make it too expensive for them to stay there, make the cost too high. It will not be easy, but with George W's help, anything is possible.

(I am remembering an English nanny I had at home, when I was about three or four. She taught me several English nursery rhymes, including:

Georgie Porgie pudding and pie,
Kiss the girls and made them cry,
When the boys came out to play,
Georgie Porgie ran away.

That's great! It's a perfect nickname for you know who.)

December 14.

Pervaiz Musharraf has survived another attempt on his life! I am beginning to suspect that Allah is protecting him. How can that be? The man slips past suicide bombers like a jackal in the night. It is not possible that anyone can be so lucky.

December 18.

Prosecutors in California have charged Michael Jackson with seven counts of child molestation. Hearings are scheduled for early next year.

Ayman is looking positively ill with worry, quite stricken, with a haunted look in the eyes. And if anyone mentions Jackson, he will immediately leap to the singer's defense. I imagine he must be expecting the public prosecutors to lay similar charges at his door in the near future.

Maybe I should send them a dossier? I could do it anonymously. He'd never know. It would be a great way of getting rid of him. Of course, if I chose to do it openly it would set me up in front of the world as a staunch defender of moral standards.

December 21.

"The American soldier" has been named as TIME magazine's "Person of the Year." I mean, why don't they just come out and admit that the magazine is written by White House staff, edited by Cheney and Rumsfeld, and printed in the basement of the west wing?

I am still furious they never chose me as "Man of the Year" in 2001. How PC was that! What moral cowards they were to have voted for that New York mayor—whose name I now cannot even remember. I mean, did he "for better or worse, most influence events in the preceding year"? Reality check, please!

Other so-called "baddies," like Hitler and Stalin, have made it onto the cover, so why not me? I have written to the editor to complain. Fat lot of good it's going to do me, I suspect, but they may at least publish my letter. Then people will know how I feel about the snub—because that is what it is, a snub, pure and simple. I think they're being very petty, not to say mean-spirited.

December 24.

I am surrounded by people who seem determined to make my life hell. I sometimes think they are totally unappreciative of everything that I have to do, and are intent solely on placing obstacles in my path.

Take this morning. I sat down to breakfast with the others. When I opened my tub of yoghurt (clearly labeled OSAMA), I found half a dozen goat droppings floating on the surface of the cream. I looked up and Ali was just staring at me, his head tilted to one side, a slight smile on his face, obviously wondering how I would react. He didn't say anything, didn't do anything, simply sat and stared at me. I knew it was him. I almost threw the yoghurt in his face, but even with Abu in the room I wasn't too confident of my chances if he became really mad. So, with what I thought was commendable dignity, I stood up and, without saying a word, dropped the tub of yoghurt amongst the pile of rubbish in the corner of the cave, and walked out, head held high. I certainly wasn't going to give him the satisfaction of creating a scene.

Then to crown my day, Abu and I walked into the cave this afternoon and found Ayman and Omar lying on a blanket in each other's arms, stark naked. Omar almost died of embarrassment being caught like that, but the Doctor just smiled at me as if he didn't give a damn (he's another Ali, that one: a degenerate nutcase.) I've long suspected there was something going on between those two, and now I know for sure. I wish I didn't.

Abu made the situation worse by standing next to me and saying, over and over again, "Hey, what are you guys doing? What's up?" I told him to shut up. I sometimes think he hasn't discovered sex yet, despite his devouring of numerous porn magazines, and believes babies are delivered by a stork or something.

December 25.

What a terrible Christmas present. Pervaiz Musharraf has survived another attempt on his life! That's two in as many weeks. This is getting boring. The man is protected by someone up there—surely it cannot be Allah! He leads a charmed life, that's for sure.

Without drawing attention to it, but just on the off-chance that one of the men was feeling charitable, I left a stocking at the end of my bunk last night. (I know it's a heathen practice, but what's the harm if you don't believe in it.) If anyone had commented on the stocking, I was going to say casually, "Oh, that's nothing, just left it out for Samah to wash."

It's just that Mummy always gave me a stocking right up until I left home, and I do really enjoy opening it on Christmas morning. It's the most exciting part of the day, sitting up in bed, reaching down into the stocking, wondering what you will pull out next. Anyway, such a charitable thought does not seem to have occurred to anyone: the stocking was empty this morning—apart from a piece of used chewing gum.

December 28.

Emailed George the latest joke about him on the internet. He's with Queen Lizzie in London and he's telling her that he's thinking of calling America a Kingdom. She points out to him that he can't do this because he isn't a King. "How about a Principality then?" he asks her a moment later. "But you're not a Prince." Bush ponders this for a few minutes and then suggests he might refer to America as an Empire, until the Queen points out that he isn't an Emperor either. She's a little fed up by now, and says, "Mr. Bush, I think you're doing very nicely as a country." I thought it very funny, but am not too sure that he will.

December 29.

Seems George W. didn't think the joke was very funny. Received an email back today that read: "Dear Mr. bin Laden, I'm sorry, but I didn't understand that little story you sent me. Was it supposed to be funny? Yours, George." Well, what can one say?

December 30.

I still sometimes find myself thinking about Mohammed Atta. I remember when he came to Afghanistan to meet me. A strange little man, rather withdrawn and awkward. He was an architect supposedly, although I cannot imagine him designing anything grander than an outside bathroom.

Ayman and I gave him the usual spiel: "You have been chosen. It is your honor to become a martyr for Islam. The reward for your loyalty is a martyr's death."

He said nothing. Just stared at myself and Ayman as if he was trying to comprehend what we were saying to him. I think he was a little overawed meeting both of us at the same time, although it was likely to have been my presence, primarily, that overwhelmed him (my deputy not having what you could really call a forceful personality.)

After a few moments he said: "You mean, commit suicide?"

"That is a word we do not to use around here, Atta. We prefer to call it self-martyrdom."

I knew all about the man, about his drinking and fornicating, and his rather nasty predisposition to beating up prostitutes. But I wasn't too fussy about who we used at the end of the day. Just so long as we could find some suckers who were willing to fly jets into buildings, I'd be happy.

I cut to the chase. "You know, Atta, that a martyr, one who lays down his life in the fight against the infidel, is guaranteed to receive his reward in heaven: seventy virgin brides—"

"I thought it was seventy-two." He interrupted me quicker than a hawk swooping out of the sky.

Somewhat taken aback, I turned to Ayman: "Seventy-two, is that right, Doctor? You're the expert on these matters."

He nodded. "The boy has done his homework."

"You're sure? I always thought it was seventy." I honestly felt like saying it was more likely to be *one* seventy-two year old virgin.

"It's seventy-two, Osama, OK? Seventy-two. Don't go on about it. We have it on good authority." He glowered at me as if afraid I was about to raise doubts in Atta's mind. I didn't see what the fuss was about to be honest: what difference would two virgins make between friends?

I turned back to our disciple. "Seems I've been wrong all this time. It's seventy-two virgin brides, and they'll all be just for you, Atta. You don't even have to share them round or anything like that. They're all yours. It should make for an eternity of bliss. You could make them last for many years, just enjoying one a month, say."

"Osama!" I could see Ayman was becoming impatient. His voice was becoming dangerously quiet.

"Sorry, I was getting a little carried away…"

Atta interrupted: "I'd prefer experienced women actually, instead of virgins, if that's possible."

Ayman and I looked at each other, not believing our ears.

"It's just that I don't want to have to teach them what to do. I want them to show me…Well, you know, *things, tricks.*"

"Of course, yes, I understand," I said, "very sensible. But I think they only supply virgins. I'm not sure they have anything else in stock, so to speak."

Ayman leapt in quickly: "I'm sure we can put in a request for experienced women instead of virgins, if that's your preference, Atta. Don't worry about it; rest assured it will be arranged."

"Now, Atta," I continued, "it is also true that should you die fighting the Americans, then you will receive twice as many rewards as you would if you were to die fighting any another country. Don't ask me why that should be so, but it is."

"Double rewards? Are those like frequent flyer points?" he asked. It was easy to see he'd been living in the States for a few years.

Ayman leapt in, probably terrified at what I might say. "Yes, in a way they are, Atta, excellent way of putting it. They're very similar to frequent flyer points. Same principle."

"I've got a lot of frequent flyer points already," Atta said, "so that's great if I can add to them." He grinned at us, suddenly quite cheerful.

"I'm sure you'll earn frequent flyer points on your last flight, too. But, of course, that's a separate issue." I was finding it difficult to believe this man. Where on earth had Ayman found him? I tried to get back on track: "And on top of that," I continued, "your family will receive $30,000."

"American dollars?"

"Yes."

"Definitely American dollars?"

"Yes."

"But why will I receive money?"

It wasn't a question I had anticipated. "Well, obviously as a kind of thank you. Yes, that's it, a thank you for services rendered."

"But what can I do with $30,000?"

"As I said, it will go to your family."

Ayman interrupted, at his avuncular best: "You will hardly need any money in Paradise, Atta."

"Exactly, you'll be too busy with the virgins. Another advantage of virgins over experienced women, of course, is that you won't need money to take them out to dinner or to a drive-in or to anything like that. Virgins aren't like normal women. They'll be grateful enough just to be…well, serviced, if you follow my drift."

"Osama!"

"Ayman, I'm just trying to explain things to Atta, to make things absolutely clear. And listen to this, Atta: and there's more! Just like they say in the commercials: and there's more! As well as a set of steak knives—no, no, I'm kidding! But this is true: as well as the virgins—or experienced women—and the money, you will be spared through your self-martyrdom both the Last Judgement *and* the Punishment of the Grave. What do you think of that?"

To be honest, he didn't look too impressed.

"That's a good deal, Atta, believe me, a very good deal. But just to convince you, we'll throw in some steak knives as well."

Ayman was beginning to look upset. Luckily, I was rescued by Atta—I say luckily, but it was in fact a really curly question. "Why aren't you performing self-martyrdom yourself if this is such a good deal?"

He was looking right at me, but I decided to play for time; I needed a few minutes to think of an answer. "Who? Me or al-Zawahiri?"

"Either of you."

I took a deep breath. "That is a good question, Atta, a very good question. To be honest, it is such a good question, why don't I let Ayman answer that one for you."

"As Osama said, that is indeed a good question, an excellent question, and yet the answer is very simple." Ayman, however, had to stare at the floor for a few moments before he could think of this very simple answer. "It is, of course, because we are both already guaranteed a place in Paradise thanks to our battles with the Russians in Afghanistan. Now we would like others to have the opportunity to go straight to Paradise. It would be wrong of Osama and me to be selfish in such matters."

Atta shrugged. He still did not look too impressed.

"We are both very jealous of the honor that has befallen you," I said. "What would we give to be in your shoes! Often I wake up in the morning and think: Oh I would be so happy if I could be a martyr today! I hope the infidels find me and kill me before the sun sets. And doubtless Ayman thinks the same way, too. Indeed, you are a very lucky man, Atta. I hope you appreciate that."

Without giving him a chance to reply, I went on to explain the plot to him. I gave him as much detail as he would need, no more. Ayman and I had worked out everything very carefully over the recent months, and Atta was to be the one who, with the help of Khalid, would make it all happen. To be honest, I had my doubts about the man in the early days, but Ayman had reassured me.

"He is exactly the type of man we're looking for, Osama: a misfit, violent, brought up without a father. He has weak family and social support. He is disillusioned with his life. He is underemployed. He is sexually frustrated and envious of the sexual freedom of others. He is anally retentive, angry and obsessive. He feels disfranchised, and hates the West as much as he loves it. He certainly does not have a mind of his own."

"He's like most of our followers then, is that what you're saying?"

"Yes."

"When you put it like that, he sounds perfect." And he did, too.

Because Ayman is a psychiatrist, I bowed to his judgment in this matter, even though I have never known a sane psychiatrist in my life. He did, in the long run, turn out to be exactly right. (I'm always the first to admit when someone else proves me wrong. It's one of my main leadership qualities.)

"Now one other thing, Atta," I said.

He looked up. There was a haunted look about him, and I saw that his hands were shaking. We'd better get him a drink, I thought. I'm sure there's a bottle of whisky somewhere. I even considered giving him one of my precious Valiums, but decided that would be far too generous.

"Yes?" I could hear the fear in his voice.

"Atta, only you and five others will know that they are to be blessed with martyrdom. You six are the important ones, the true martyrs."

"What of the others?"

"Well, they're going to get a big surprise." I laughed.

Ayman tutted.

"No, I'm sorry, what I meant was, the other thirteen—unlucky thirteen, you see!—will be told it's just a normal, everyday hijacking, the kind of thing they probably do every week. All they need to think is that their plane, once they have control of it, will land at some airport or other, where negotiations will take place. It doesn't matter what the negotiations are for; just tell them there will be some."

"Will they go to Paradise, too?"

"Oh I'm sure they will."

"But they won't get seventy-two virgins, will they?"

I could hear in his question the answer he was hoping for (I'm quick at picking up things like that.)

"Good heavens, no, Atta, absolutely not. Possibly just one or two—if that, if they're lucky. They certainly don't deserve any more than that."

We chose well. Nineteen young men laid down their lives for a total of one thousand three hundred and sixty-eight virgins. I reckon Allah got something of a bargain there. (To be honest, I didn't realize there were that many virgins still around.)

Mind you, those idiots who let themselves be overpowered and crashed the plane into a field in Pennsylvania, I don't think they should get seventy-two virgins. I think half that number would be fairer. It's true they lay down their lives, but they weren't successful, so I don't think they should get their full reward. In fact, maybe they deserve just a dozen.

I only wish they'd made it to the White House. That would have been the crowning glory—especially if Bush had been at home. But there again, maybe not. I could have ended up with someone much worse as President. Like Cheney.

December 31.

Sometimes I will spend the evening watching old Woody Allen films. My favorite is *Bananas*. But I also like *Annie Hall*, and many of his other films.

I don't believe the man is Jewish, although he goes on about it often enough, basing all his humor around his Jewishness. But imagining being Jewish would be easy enough for anyone to do, even though it would be a nightmarish scenario.

The man couldn't be that talented a director and writer if he was Jewish, so he's obviously lying. And if in the unlikely event he was telling the truth, well, I wouldn't look at any of his films. No way.

2004

January 4.

I had the following conversation with Mohammed today.

"It's the time of year for giving, for thinking of others," I said to him.

"Praise be to Allah."

"Indeed, praise be to Allah." After a short pause I continued, but more warily: "It is the time for thinking of those who are less fortunate than ourselves." He nodded. To what extent could I labor the point, I wondered. Staring pointedly across the cave at Samah who was preparing the evening meal, I added meaningfully: "To think of those who have nothing, who are possibly alone, who…must…do…without."

But Mohammed just sat beside me on the floor of the cave, nodding and smiling, agreeing with everything I said, without understanding what I was driving at.

"I am deprived, Mohammed, I am lonely, I am one who must do without." I'm not sure what affect I was having on him, but I was practically reducing myself to tears.

He turned and looked at me. I turned and looked at his wife, then turned back to him, expectation in my eyes—alongside the tears. He said: "Allah be praised that these trials are sent to each of us so that we may learn to do His will."

"Indeed," I said, going suddenly limp.

Soon I think I must join Ali and start doing the business with a goat. Horrible thought.

January 12.

Don't underestimate Cheney. Don't even misunderestimate him. This is the man who is reputed to have received no less than five deferments between 1963 and 1966 in order to avoid being sent to Vietnam. That is some achievement.

He suddenly decided to go to college—deferment 1. Then he went to university—deferment 2. He applied for another deferment while at university—deferment 3. He even got married—deferment 4. On receiving news that childless married men would no longer be exempt, he rushed straight into the bedroom, impregnated his wife…Phew, just in time!—and received deferment 5.

It certainly shows what a scheming, cunning man he is!

January 20.

The turncoat! I cannot believe it, Colonel Qaddafi has sold out. Once the scourge of the West, once No. 1 on America's most wanted list, once the living nightmare of every Christian on the planet, and he's chucked it all in to become Mr. Nice Guy. How pathetic is that. I used to look up to him and admire him for sponsoring terrorism around the world when I was growing up in the 1970s. Instead of listening to Cat Stevens, the Bee Gees and Michael Jackson in my teenage years, Qaddafi was the ideal to which I aspired. Now he's obviously become old, and gone soft in the head. Truth is, I've always had my suspicions about his mental state.

Not only has he now agreed to pay millions of dollars to the families of the victims of the Lockerbie disaster, but he has promised to destroy all of his nuclear warheads and WMDs. And for what? So that he can trade with his old enemies, that's why. He's sacrificed everything just so he can export some goats' cheese, yak butter and sand clocks, or whatever it is his Country produces, and import some TV sets and refrigerators. Has the man no principles at all?

I really find the whole thing quite unbelievable. But maybe some good will come out of it. Have told Ayman to get in touch with the old traitor and see if we can't do a deal over his now unwanted nuclear warheads, before they're carted off to the tip. It could be the opportunity we've been waiting for. And surely he'll agree to a deal for old time's sake, because we were once fellow terrorists.

In a small private ceremony—just myself in other words—I removed his signed portrait from the wall of my cave, where it was positioned alongside those of Fidel Castro, Kim Jong-il, Mugabe, Khomeini, the one-eyed cleric, and an extremely rare autographed Pol Pot portrait. My Gallery of Heroes is diminishing.

(Nearby, as a kind of sideshow, I also have portraits of Ronald Reagan and Margaret Thatcher for giving me such valuable financial support in my battle against the Soviets in Afghanistan, and of Clinton for helping us in the battle against the Serbs in Bosnia. I owe them all.)

January 23.

Displaying my usual cunning and advanced strategic thinking, I sent the following email to Pervaiz Musharraf: *Hi Perv, how's it going? I don't think it's right that you and I carry on with our senseless hostilities, so I'm suggesting we get together to discuss areas of mutual cooperation. How about we meet at* (here I put the street address of an al-Qaeda safe house in Islamabad)? *I'll be in town on January 25th so why don't we meet there for lunch? Don't bother to reply if these arrangements are convenient for you. Your affectionate brother in Islam, Osama.*

January 25.

I wish I could blow up one of those NASA rovers that are now on Mars. An opportunity to blow up the Opportunity would not go amiss. Think how much that would upset the infidels.

January 26.

Musharaff is cleverer than I thought. He didn't turn up at the safe house for lunch, so my men had to dismantle the bomb.

January 28.

They've published the Hutton Report in the UK, and this has exonerated Blair. This pleases me. I've been worried about Cherie. She has been looking so stressed recently, at times quite drawn and pale—a look that has a certain appeal, but only if one is a Romantic. I can imagine those black lines beneath her eyes are the result of sleepless nights. It's probably because those awful tabloid newspapers have been giving her, and her husband, a hard time. They are quite merciless.

Maybe I should send her a message: say how pleased I am that it has worked out well for her family. She might be surprised by my consideration. She may even contemplate doing the business with me after that. Who knows, gratitude is a powerful emotion—and Laura need never know (the news would devastate her.) From what I understand, the two ladies rarely communicate with each other and like each other even less.

February 1.

Such a tragedy. 251 pilgrims performing the Hajj were crushed to death in a stampede in Mina, outside the holy city of Mecca. I shall pray for them, the poor innocents.

February 2.

Another crisis. Omar came rushing into the cave this morning as I was about to leave for another command center with Abu. He took me aside. It seems he was down in the village of Barikot, buying up essentials (toilet paper, Coca Cola, crisps, chewing gum and such like), when he was confronted by an angry mob. It turns out Ayman has been misbehaving again: he has been interfering with a small boy from the village.

The boy claims it has been going on for some time, but his parents have only just found out. The villagers have expressed a desire to castrate my deputy, and that's just for starters. Omar's manhood only survived intact because he promised to speak to me about the matter and vowed that justice would be done and be seen to be done. It's all very well for him to make promises like that!

I phoned Ayman immediately (he's in Pakistan at the moment), and at first he denied everything. After a little while he said, "So what?" and admitted that it was true. I swore at him down the phone (something I would hesitate doing if he was there in the flesh. You can't be too careful with these psychopaths.)

I am now more convinced than ever that this is why he was forced to leave Egypt in 1986. Many parents were planning to bring charges of pedophilia against him, and he realized he would have to get out or suffer the consequences.

The long and the short of it is that I had to go down to the village with Omar this evening. It was not a good night to be out: it was snowing heavily and our horses had problems keeping to the path. They were virtually white-out conditions.

I visited the family—making sure no one else was in attendance. Once I arrived on the scene, they became, as I expected they would, very quiet and respectful. They were obviously quite overcome by my presence—not surprisingly, I guess. The father, a gray-bearded old man with one fine tooth at the front, and top, of his mouth, was almost struck dumb. This made my task easier. He insisted on calling me *loar sheik*(8) and on pouring me endless cups of tea. Nothing was too much trouble. If I'd asked for permission to take his young son away with me, I'm certain he would have agreed.

When I proposed that he accept $US5,000 a year for life (more than he'd made in his lifetime as likely as not) if he dropped the matter, he fell to his knees as if it was he who was asking forgiveness. Such was his gratitude, he kissed the hem of my robe as well as my hand, that he also shook for several minutes. He was very dirty, obviously having never washed, and I tried to disengage my hand as quickly as possible, then wiped it surreptitiously on my robe.

I immediately wished that my terms had been less generous, but consoled myself with the thought that a few years down the track we will probably be able to quietly shelve the whole matter anyway—if the old fool hasn't already died.

I only hope Ayman hasn't been doing this in every village along the Afghanistan-Pakistan border. It will cost us a fair bit of money if he has—and could even lose us support. He assures me he hasn't, though I'm not sure I believe him. Never trust a psychopath, nor a pedophile, that's my motto.

Omar and I spent the night with a family in the same village. They are cousins or friends of Abu's, I believe. The father and his two sons smoked opium all night and I couldn't get a word of sense out of any of them. I'm convinced the man's toothless, grinning wife was flirting with me, in quite a brazen manner, but it may only have been because she was cross-eyed.

We spent the night on the floor, squashed between the family's goats. I thanked Allah that Ali wasn't with us, although I doubt we'd have been expected to pay compensation if he'd interfered with any of those creatures—unlike Ayman and the human *kid*. Ha, ha.

February 4.

Some Pakistani scientist named Dr Khan has admitted selling nuclear secrets to Libya, Iran and North Korea. It makes me sick. What has the world come to! Just who can I trust, who can I rely on? This idiot must have known I would be happy to buy those secrets off him, too. Why on earth did he leave me out? I've had the word out on the street for a year or two now that we are "in the market" for all things nuclear, and yet this man of science must have the mind of a goat herder, a simpleton, obviously without sufficient little gray cells in his tiny brain to think of contacting us, his obvious market. What a moron he must be. His so-called "secrets" are probably not worth the paper they're printed on. When you think about it, strictly speaking, a Pakistani nuclear bomb is an oxymoron.

Fools such as this scientist are ruining my health. My nerves are shot to pieces. I take Valium several times a day now. If someone shook me, I'm sure I'd rattle.

February 15.

One of those brilliantly clear, sunny days you sometimes get in these parts. Not a cloud in the sky, the surrounding snow-covered peaks of the Hindu Kush standing crystal clear against the blue, and the air so sharp it takes one's breath away.

But, hey, I'm not English (thanks be to Allah!), so must resist the temptation to spend the day discussing the weather. On to more important matters...

It is a waste of time and energy thinking about it, I know, but I do wish that Georgie Porgie had been at his desk (is he *ever* at his desk?) in the White House on September 11, and that the fourth jet had made it that far.

But then I console myself by thinking how lucky we are to have him as President. Imagine if Cheney had been forced to step in, how awful that would have been. Bushy may be stupid—no, no, he is *definitely* stupid—but Cheney, he is mad, really crazy. And that's far more dangerous.

Bush always looks to me like a kid who has been caught by his parents doing something he shouldn't be doing. I can see him standing there in his shorts and open-neck shirt, his muddy knees, socks around his ankles, and hands behind his back, protesting his innocence. He has those raised eyebrows and those wide open eyes, and an intensely earnest expression. He looks as if he is lying or, in the language of a child, telling a fib. It is almost possible to hear him saying, "What, *me?!* No, Mum, no, Dad, I didn't do it, honestly. It must have been Jeb."

February 20.

Aymed complained this morning about not having slept because he was so cold. He looked meaningfully at me as he said it. I'm not denying that he loaned me two of his blankets when I complained about how cold I was at night, but as I said to him:

"Which is better: that I am warm and have a good night's sleep while you, a common foot soldier, suffer a little discomfort? Or that you are warm while I, the driving force behind al-Qaeda, the leader of our men and the promoter of our cause around the world, sleep only fitfully, waking up in the morning incapable of carrying out my onerous duties because I am too tired and have also caught a cold?"

Of course, he had no answer probably because he didn't understand what I was saying, but still he stormed out of the cave without a word to any of us. I swear that if there had been a door he would have slammed it. None of the others said anything, but carried on with what they were doing, although one or two of them did look at me in a way I did not like.

February 21.

Fazul arrived today to fix my computer. The Americans have just placed a $2 million reward on his head, so he is feeling mightily pleased with himself. "But I've a long way to go before I catch up with you, Sheikh."

I smiled modestly, but he's right. Another $23 million to be exact.

Like every IT expert I have ever met, he has a somewhat clinical demeanor, and glasses. I sometimes imagine that the inside of his head must be like the inside of a computer.

He certainly knows his business. He sits at my laptop striking the keys so fast, and clicking the mouse with such speed, I am unable to keep track of the websites and symbols that flash up on the screen. He is like my son, Tariq, in this respect. Like all teenagers, Tariq can operate computers without any effort at all. He understands everything about them. And, like Fazul, he seems to access parts of the computer I did not even know existed.

It is strange to welcome him into the cave. I feel like Napoleon greeting one of his generals. Because that is what Fazul is at the end of the day. Although he is an IT expert, he is one of my generals in the war we are fighting. Increasingly, this war is being waged in cyber space.

It was he who showed me how to scan photographs from porn magazines (Abu has a good supply which I periodically find him masturbating over), post them into obscure, pre-arranged websites or chat rooms, and then, using steganography, embed secret messages or maps into them. They are almost impossible to spot, and in the unlikely event they are spotted, it's even more unlikely they could ever be deciphered. We also scramble messages to our overseas operatives, using encryption.

The FBI has publicly admitted they are behind the eight ball when it comes to competing with al-Qaeda in cyberspace. Personally, I'd put them further back than that (although I have no idea what this "eight ball" is.)

February 27.

I am convinced, utterly convinced, she would love me if she knew the *real* me. It's an affinity I feel we have, a conjunction of souls. I believe it is possible to look a woman in the eyes and you just *know*. You know there's something between you. And there is between us, between Laura and me. I wonder if she has ever looked at my photograph and thought the same. I would not be at all surprised. Maybe she has a framed photograph of me hidden away in a chest-of-drawers, beneath her clothes—maybe in her underwear drawer! Now wouldn't that be a place for me to spend the day—and she looks at it when her cowboy husband is out chopping down trees on his ranch or clearing the brush around their homestead. (This seems to be a favorite pastime of his, the significance of which I fail to understand. Possibly it makes him feel masculine. But it's also a mindless task, so it obviously suits him.)

I already have four wives, and know that those stupid Christians believe in only having one, but I have given serious consideration to making Laura my number one wife. That would be a singular honor for her.

I could get rid of Fatima somehow, although Om might raise some objection. Laura wouldn't be my only wife, but she would be my first wife, and wouldn't that be enough to tempt her to leave George?

I certainly have one worry about her: her lack of stature. She is only five foot two inches, which is a good deal smaller than me. Would this present us with problems—especially in what my friends, the French, call the *boudoir*? Perhaps it would make us more innovative.

She has her own web page. She obviously has many admirers, many fans. I have left messages there for her, not using my real name of course, but a clever pseudonym: Sam.

I know she will not reply to my messages if she discovers who I am—she has been too well brain-washed for that. But if I had time to work on her, I'm sure I could persuade her. She may be a clever woman, she's a librarian after all, but I still don't believe she knows her own mind right now.

All visitors to her website are invited to leave a message, so I did so. I took special care with it.

There is one who awaits you. Dark, brooding presence with international reputation. Physically and mentally honed, extremely good looking and successful. Offers you a life out of the ordinary, with excitement and challenges galore. Likes reading, walking, guns, The Simpsons, *and eating out. Please reply. You will never regret it.*

She did not reply. I can only hope she regrets it—one day. I imagine she does not reply to messages from anyone. She probably gets too much mail to make replying practicable. I am disappointed nevertheless, but not despairing. Time is on my side—as we always say in al-Qaeda.

February 29.

This evening was the last day of viewing that self- and sexually-obsessed foursome. The final episode of *Sex in the City* was, well, somewhat predictable. Miranda, my favorite, and Samantha fell in love—but, no, not with each other. Now that would have been something else, that would have been worth watching! Charlotte adopted a Chinese girl (ho hum, how PC is that!), and Carrie ran into Big in Paris just after she left her artist boyfriend. Of course, he declared his love (how many times has he done that!) and we're supposed to believe they ended up living happily ever after—or until he goes off with someone else, more likely.

Don't know what I will do on Wednesday evenings from now on. The series certainly portrayed the emptiness of life in the West (with no one able to raise their eyes higher than their Manolos or lift their thoughts higher than the bed), but it was nevertheless fascinating to watch—like staring at bored monkeys in the zoo; their shenanigans are interesting, even though puerile and meaningless.

March 2.

John Kerry has become the Democratic presidential nominee. Oh dear, I hope he won't beat Georgie Porgie. What will I do if that should happen? However, it doesn't seem likely that a man who has made his fortune from marrying a woman in baked beans could make it as far as the White House—unless he blows there under his own steam, of course! Mind you, second rate Hollywood stars can make it as far as the White House, so why not the husband of a baked bean heiress?

March 8.

Hearings into 9/11 have started in the US. They want to discover how they could have avoided letting it happen. I should write and tell them: they couldn't have done anything. But I will let them get on with it—it will give them something to do.

March 10.

Happy birthday to me! No cake, no presents (although Abu did offer me one of his old, rusty chest expanders), not even breakfast in bed. Not surprisingly, I sometimes wonder if anyone cares. I whispered to Samah when Mohammed went out of the cave after dinner that, if she was feeling generous, she could give me a very special present for my birthday that wouldn't cost her anything at all. She tutted in a disapproving fashion, and walked away without a word.

March 11.

There were 911 days between 9/11 and today, when the Madrid bombs went off. That's typical of Mustafa Setmariam Nasar (or Abu Musab al-Suri as he prefers to be called)—totally anal. He's so obviously trying to hitch a ride on my coat tails.

I never liked the man. When he was training at the al-Ghuraba camp, he tried to treat me as an equal. I soon put paid to that. I won't have the likes of him eating out of my rice bowl.

He dyes his hair red, and has this habit of always patting it to make sure it's in place. He's so vain, checking himself in a small mirror he carries around with him every few minutes. He's quite shameless about it, producing the mirror from his backpack right in front of everyone and then preening himself quite openly. He's not even good looking, certainly not in the same league as myself.

Even though we trained him to fight the infidel, he never does any of the dirty work himself. Oh no! He skulks away in some flat or other, always ensuring he has plenty of good food (he eats caviar like other people eat peanuts) and bottles of quality wine at hand, then sends his minions off to do the dangerous work. He excuses this behavior by saying he is the brains of the operation, and is therefore too important to put himself at risk. But I know the truth: he's a sniveling coward, and he's too in love with the good life to risk being killed. I absolutely refuse to send him any money or help him out in any way. He's not going to enjoy the good life at my expense.

I remember when he was at the Kandahar training camp, where we first met. He was slightly wounded; it was a flesh wound, the slightest nick, caused by some incompetent recruit firing his rifle by mistake. And Nasar was screaming as if his wound was mortal, more shame that it wasn't! Clutching his side, he was rolling around on the ground shouting, "Save me! Someone help me! I'm bleeding to death."

In fact there was barely any blood to be seen, and it wasn't too long before some of the men started to laugh at him and his pathetic carryings-on. This set him off crying. While he was being patched up he was sobbing, "You guys are really mean, you don't know what it's like to be shot"—this to men, some of whose bodies were scarred and pitted all over by bullet wounds! But it wasn't too long before he was strutting around the camp boasting of the time he had "escaped the jaws of death" and "been ready to enter Paradise as a martyr."

I'm glad I'm not like that. I'm glad I've got guts. I'm ready, willing and able to get out there with my men, and stand shoulder-to-shoulder with them as we fight the enemy in hand-to-hand combat. But then I'm a man. Whereas I have my doubts about the chromosomal balance of that creature whom I have been informed is now skulking in some Tunis hotel, buried under a pile of nubile flesh.

March 18.

News has just come in that the Doctor was almost captured by the Pakistan army. There again, so many people are *almost* captured by the Pakistan army, it beggars description. Those dunderheads wouldn't be able to get their hands on a mountain goat if both its front and back legs were trussed up with rope and it had been tied to a stake in the ground (with Ali lying on top of it!)

The good Doctor was holed up in a remote area of western Pakistan and awoke one morning to find himself and his followers surrounded. At this moment in time, it looks as if one of his own men betrayed him.

The battle raged for several days, with many lives lost on both sides. It was during the fighting—but not before, I understand—that the Pakistanis discovered Ayman was in their net, and immediately Musharref boasted to the world's media that they were about to capture al-Qaeda's second-in-command. More fool him, counting his chickens before they've hatched. Musharref does not appreciate how many sympathizers we have within his Government and Armed Forces, and when he leaked this information to the world's press, he alerted those supporters for us. And that's what let Ayman off the hook.

A Pakistani army sympathizer allowed the Doctor and one of his operatives to slip through the net in the middle of the night, and they managed to make it across the border into Afghanistan.

I'm not sure how Ayman would have coped with so much excitement. He's none too fit. In fact I'd go so far as to call him portly. He has enough problems walking between command centers when time is not of the essence, but with the Pakistani army on his tail, in winter, I can imagine how trying it must have been for his colleague to get him across those mountain passes. He'd have been moaning continuously, his spectacles would have been covered in ice, and he'd have been complaining—as he always does—about his chilblains. Some doctor! Heal thyself.

My feelings about his escape are ambivalent. Quite honestly, I'd be more than pleased to see the back of him, so long as there were a few bullets in it, but there is one slight problem: he is my medical practitioner. He knows my medical history and my aches and pains better than anyone, so should he be captured or killed, I would be left very much to my own devices.

There aren't any other doctors round here—unless one of the local herdsmen happens to be hiding his light under a bushel. I know of doctors in the Sudan and in Saudi Arabia, but I suspect none of them would be willing to give up lucrative careers in order to come and live out here and be hunted by the Americans.

There's a doctor in Kabul to whom I was once introduced, but he's an abortionist as well as a heroin addict, so I'm a little reluctant to entrust my wellbeing to him.

I understand Ayman is still with us, so I shouldn't worry too much at this stage. But I fear he's likely to be even more insufferable than usual boasting about his close escape from the enemy. We are to meet up in a couple of days in the Helmand district, and discuss tactics.

March 22.

The Israelis have assassinated the founder and spiritual leader of Hamas, Shaik Ahmad Yassin. Blind, wheelchair-bound, scarcely capable of lifting a finger and in his late sixties, he of course made the perfect target for the Israelis. I never knew the man, but he sounded like a good person. (If the Israelis hated him so much, he must have been.)

March 26.

I was thinking about my father today.

He had his heart in the right place, even though he made so many mistakes in his life. The way he put himself at the beck and call of the Royal Family still disgusts me. He did well out of it, certainly, but I don't think he should have demeaned himself like that.

If only I had got to know him better. Being only ten when he died, we had little time together. Only some camping trips into the desert with my other siblings—and often those of the Royal Family as well. Always other people around.

I think he was always displeased with me, seeing me as too bookish. The fact that he fell out with Mummy did not help. She was far too strong and outspoken for him.

Apart from Al-Khalifa, his first and favorite wife, and the only one who ever stood up to him, the other wives were always happy to go along with whatever he said or wanted. Mummy wouldn't accept this, however, and that is why he eventually banished her to the provinces.

I think he should have made more of an effort with her, if only for my sake. And she with him, too. Both of them were too selfish and forgot my needs.

I sometimes wonder what he would think of my fame now. Would he be proud, or would he disown me like the rest of the family? He was an old-fashioned Muslim in many ways—in most ways—only too eager to kowtow to the west.

Perhaps he would not have been proud of me. None of my brothers or sisters speak to me now, not since Holy Tuesday(9), and even Mummy speaks to me differently. Our conversations have become stilted, like two strangers who have just met in a coffee shop. My wives never say anything about the New York and Washington raids, but then it's not right that they should. But it hurts me sometimes that Mummy is not more understanding. I'd have thought most parents would be proud to have me as their son.

April 4.

Just as I predicted, Mustafa Setmariam Nasar ran out on his colleagues who carried out the Madrid bombings. Jamal Zougam, Serhane Abdelmaji (known as the Tunisian), and Jamal Ahmidan (known as the Chinese) were cornered in an apartment in the city yesterday, and blew themselves up rather than surrender to the police. They are real heroes.

Nasar however, according to my sources, is lying by the pool in some five star hotel in Tunis, probably with two or three teenage girls waiting to entertain him when he returns to his room. That's the only kind of paradise that man's interested in. He's probably been showing them his "war wound" and recounting how he fought hundreds of the infidel single-handed. Perhaps he'll have a pillow fight with the girls. That's about all he's capable of.

April 6.

I phoned Mummy this evening. It always puts me in a bad mood. I so look forward to speaking to her and giving her all my news, but invariably we end up arguing.

When one of her servants eventually got her to the phone, she didn't say, "Hello, darling, how are you?" or "Hello, Osama, how lovely to hear from you," she just launched straight into: "And how are my grandchildren?" There was no polite introductory remarks, no brief civility, she just pitched straight in with, "And how are my grandchildren?"

I almost put the phone down; it's more than flesh and blood can bear. What about me? Does she not care? I need affection too, I need some love. It was obvious that I was going to have to make a superhuman effort.

"They're all well, thank you, Mummy. They send you their love."

This was a lie. I hadn't spoken to any of my children for weeks, and whenever I did speak to them they never asked after their granny.

I realized I hadn't planned our conversation sufficiently, and that it was already going off the rails. All I could think to tell her about the children was Mohammed's wedding.

"Did it go well? I wish I had been able to be there for my grandson's wedding." This was said as if it was my fault.

"You could have been, Mummy."

"Oh yes, the Americans are going to let me fly to Afghanistan to see my own son, number one on their most wanted list, and my grandson. How likely is that!"

"We could have arranged something." I couldn't imagine what. "Ali made a wonderful speech. Did you hear?"

"Did I hear! The whole world heard. Imagine asking a ten year old to make a political speech at his own brother's wedding."

"He wanted to do it, Mummy. He insisted."

"It was probably no more than trying to earn his father's love. They say history repeats itself."

"And what's that supposed to mean?"

"Nothing."

There was a long silence. I wondered if anyone was listening in. Seeing that I was in a callbox in Kandahar, it didn't really matter if they were.

"That's no life for my grandchildren, that's all I'm saying. What kind of childhood are they having? They should be allowed to come home and live with me. They would be safe here, and properly looked after."

"They're well looked after here, Mummy."

"Are they? What about their education?"

"They go to school in Kandahar."

"School in Kandahar! I can imagine. Who teaches them: an Afghan yak herder? And what are they studying: poppy farming?"

"That's being unfair."

"Is it?"

"Anyway, I've told you before, Saudi Arabia will never be their home while the Americans are there."

She ignored me—she always does when it suits her. "My grandchildren aren't living with that horrible one-eyed cleric, are they?"

"Mullah Omar is a nice man, Mummy. You've never met him. He's very kind."

She snorted. "Very kind? Oh yes, I'm sure he is. I understand he's fond of little children."

"That's Ayman al-Zawahiri. You're getting two people muddled."

"Well, I hope they never stay with him, whatever his name is."

"They hardly ever see Ayman, Mummy. He's usually in the mountains with me."

"Well, I hope you don't let him interfere with you, Osama!" She sounded quite shocked.

"He likes children, Mummy. I'm too old for him."

"Just as well. But you can never be too careful with people like that. I would suggest you sleep with a gun by your side—just in case. Those kind of people are quite depraved; they'll try and have their way with anyone they can lay their hands on."

"Yes, Mummy."

"And I hope you keep an eye on the children when he's around, that Ayman what's his face?"

"Of course I do. Not that he would harm them." I banged the side of the phone box with my fist. Allah, give me patience!

"What's that noise?"

"It must have been someone in the street." I ground my teeth.

Conversation is never easy when I phone home. There is not too much we can talk about. She tells me a little about the family, although she rarely speaks to any of them now, nor they to her, but there's little I can tell her about my life. She's hardly going to ask, "And how's work going? Did you bomb any buildings this week? How many people did you kill today?"

She interrupted my thoughts by suddenly saying, "You were such a nice boy once, Osama."

"I beg your pardon?"

"You heard me. I don't know where we went wrong."

"Maybe you didn't go wrong, Mummy." I told myself to be patient.

"Maybe I didn't go wrong!" she shouted down the phone. "He says, maybe I didn't go wrong."

I realized she was speaking to someone at her end of the line, and momentarily panicked. "Who's there, Mummy? Who's with you?"

"It's Adiva, my best friend. She says to say hello. Wait a moment..." There was a pause, then she came back on the line: "Adiva says she loved the photograph of you in the *Riyadh Times* last week. Very handsome, she says. I think you must have got your striking looks from me."

I told her to thank Adiva, but she carried straight on:

"Maybe I didn't go wrong, how can you say that? I've brought up a son who kills thousands of people, blows up innocent women and children, who's the greatest mass-murderer of our times, and he says maybe his mother didn't go wrong. How can you do this to me?" she wailed.

"Mummy, do try and understand. Those innocent people you talk about are infidels. They are non-believers, they are not even humans. Allah is grateful when they are killed. He will be happy when they're driven from the Holy Land."

I wasn't even sure she was listening. I imagined her filing her nails; I remember she always did that when she was on the phone.

There was a long sigh from the other end of the line. "Your brothers, Bakr and Yahia, they are doing so well. Did you know that? Between them they now run your father's company. They have so much money, and so much respect in the community."

"Good for them. I hope they're very happy slaving away in an office all day."

She ignored me. "You know what I think? I think your father was never there for you. He's the one I blame for all of this."

"Ask yourself why he wasn't there, Mummy." I was becoming exasperated.

"It certainly wasn't my fault, if that's what you're saying. He wasn't there for any of his children, it wasn't just you. For the girls it was not so important, but for the seventeen boys it was important. Who could you look up to if he wasn't there? Who could be your role model?"

"He called you al-'abda(10), that's all I know."

"That was nasty of him. It was quite uncalled for. And I don't like to be reminded of it, thank you."

"It was just as bad for me. I was called the son of the slave woman, bin al-'abda. All of my life I've had to live with that, Mummy, and you wonder why I'm bitter."

"But it wasn't my fault you were called that, Osama. You can't blame me for that."

"Then who can I blame?"

"Try and see it from my point of view. Your father threw me out of the house and banished me to the provinces. I've lived the whole of my life amongst peasants."

"That's only because you wouldn't shut up, because you always argued with him. You never knew your place, that was your problem, Mummy."

"I refused to kowtow like those other bitches. I have a mind of my own, Osama. You know that."

Do I ever! "Anyway, don't complain: he left you with plenty of money."

"He may have left me money, but he didn't leave me with anyone to talk to—apart from servants. And he only gave me one child, and that child deserted me to go off and wage war on the whole world."

"Mummy, don't exaggerate."

She sniffled. I knew she was crying, and I couldn't bear it. She always ended up crying. Between her tears, she said: "You've always been so extreme in what you do, Osama. What's wrong with the middle-ground for a change? You've never been one for half measures, that's for sure. It always has to be all or nothing with you."

"Maybe that's a good thing."

"It's not healthy. At school you were always the perfect student. You studied hard, you dressed neatly, you never gave your teachers a moment's grief. Then you went to university—I had such high hopes for you. But you became a playboy instead. You went completely wild: women, alcohol and all the rest. You ignored your studies."

"I never did drugs, Mummy." I tried to be positive.

"You did just about everything else from what I've heard. And then you became a religious fanatic. From a young man who never went near a mosque, you turned into a young man who lived his whole life in the mosque. And then you became anti-American; not anti-American like a normal person, but crazily anti-American, frantically anti-American, like an insane person."

She blew her nose loudly down the phone. I remained silent.

"The Americans aren't all bad, you know, Osama. I met an awfully nice Colonel at the club last weekend. He bought me a drink."

"For God's sake, Mummy!"

"For God's sake what, Osama?"

"You know I don't like you socializing with Americans."

"I don't see what harm it can do."

"What if the media find out? What then? It could ruin me, damage my reputation overnight. *Osama bin Laden's mother seen drinking with American friends.* Imagine!"

"I don't think there's anything to worry about. He's an awfully nice man, and very witty. He said he'd phone me and we could meet again."

"I'm sure he did. He's probably a CIA agent."

"What rubbish! He was genuinely interested in you—a mother can tell these things. He was asking how you were and whether we still kept in touch."

"You surprise me," I said sarcastically.

"When I told him that you were such a worry to me, you know what he said?"

"Tell me, please."

"He said, 'Don't worry, Hamida, I have a boy just like that; out all hours of the day and night, girls, parties—he even lost his license because of drink-driving.' It's nice to know other parents have their cross to bear."

"Don't use that expression, Mummy."

"He drove me home later in the evening. Said he'd call me soon and we could maybe eat out together."

"I have to go." I couldn't take any more of this. "It was good talking to you, Mummy. Take care." And I put the phone down.

I was so angry. How could she do this to me? Did she never think of anyone but herself? How could she bring herself to socialize with the infidels? It was too much.

April 7.

The Egyptian is getting on my nerves. He can be so sanctimonious. Luckily, we don't see each other too often (having the excuse of it being unwise to be in the same place together in case the Americans attack.)

I have been extremely upset—although I do my best to hide it from everyone—since the Americans raised the reward for his capture to $US25 million. This is the same reward they're offering for me, and I find it truly insulting. What has he done to deserve that? The same level of importance cannot be placed on the captain of the ship and one of the men down in the boiler room.

I sat down this afternoon and did some calculations. I made a big effort to be totally honest and objective, and I worked out that the reward for capturing or killing Ayman, taking into account his history, nationality, current activities and potential danger to the Americans, not to mention his enthusiasm for little boys, should be about $US10 million. And that was leaning on the generous side. The fact is, the figure should be more like $5 million.

I am absolutely stunned by the amount of money they have placed on his head. I appreciate they have more money than they know what to do with, but this really does illustrate their short-sightedness. And what is it going to say to the men when they hear my deputy—this Egyptian upstart—is worth the same as me, their leader? It's going to make things very awkward round here for awhile.

I am seriously considering writing to George Tenet and asking if he will consider lowering the reward for Ayman. Or, conversely, raising the reward for me to a more realistic $50 million. If I explained the predicament he has put me in, I'm sure he would do the right thing by me. Anyway, if Ayman is worth $25 million, then I'm definitely worth $50 million.

To add insult to injury, I recently saw a newspaper article—it was also on the web—that claims the Doctor is the "organizational brain" behind al-Qaeda. They say he is the man responsible for the assault on US soldiers in Somalia in 1993, for the bombings of the East African embassies in 1998 (without doubt one of my masterstrokes), and for the attack on the *USS Cole* in Yemen in 2000.

That is fiction, fantasy, total make-believe! It is more imaginative than *The Thousand and One Nights*. I am upset and insulted. At the very most, Ayman could claim, in one or two instances, to have been in the room at the time, to have been in on the discussions, but that is all. Before I know it, they'll be saying it was his idea to bomb the World Trade Center.

I am beginning to wonder if he is secretly sending out press releases, building up his image, spreading all this misinformation—in short, blowing his own trumpet at the expense of al-Qaeda. I would not put it past him. I can see it in his eyes sometimes; the shifty, devious look behind those thick glasses. I must watch him more closely. He is definitely not to be trusted.

I sometimes worry that we are too similar. Our backgrounds have much in common. He comes from a middle class medical family in Cairo, whereas I come from a successful family in Jiddah. Like me, he comes from a large family—although not as big as mine. He has two sisters and two brothers from one mother, while I have fifty-one brothers and sisters from four different mothers.

Just as my siblings have disowned me, I understand that his have disowned Ayman. His mother still talks to him, as my mother still talks to me, but that is the only contact he now has with his family. Both of our fathers were absent much of the time when we were young (maybe we should both have a good scream about that and punch some pillows together.)

His family was nowhere near as rich as mine, and yet his upbringing could definitely be described as privileged. In fact he once told me it was because his family were outsiders in Egyptian society (they were refused entry into the Maadi Sporting Club or some such nonsense) that he took up the gun. This seems a tad melodramatic to me, but it's typical of Ayman. He likes to build things up, and he's a great one for bearing grudges.

He was a psychiatrist once, and old habits die hard. He analyses himself and others all the time. I am certain he analyses me, even though he never admits to it. (If I tell him I've killed someone, for example, he will say, "Hmmm…And how does that make you feel, Osama?") He is always questioning his own motives, forever asking why he is behaving in such and such a way. He can't pick up a saddle for his horse without wondering why he is doing it. Myself, I think it's all rubbish, this psychiatry. It's only people who have too much time on their hands who have time for such nonsense. The Americans are a case in point: all that psychiatry has made them all nuts.

What I do know about Ayman, however, is that he is boring. He is *so* boring. His whole world is politics and religion, and that's it. At least I have other interests, like internet porn, soccer and synchronized swimming. He even has a mark on his forehead, just below his turban, that has been caused—so he claims—by prostrating himself in prayer for such long periods of time every day. I myself suspect that he has made the mark himself in an attempt to portray a holy image. He is far too keen to point it out to people. I'd give anything to have the opportunity to see if I could rub it off.

As for politics, he has a problem seeing beyond Egypt. "The Part I Played in the Assassination of Anwar Sadat" is his favorite topic of conversation, and he makes it blatantly clear that he considers this to be the highlight of his career—even though it happened way back in 1981.

At least I try to see everything from a world perspective: the big picture is what I always aim for. Ayman is too short-sighted for that. His view is blocked by the pyramids. Most days he can't see any further than planning to procure his next little boy. I haven't said as much to him—I'm not that stupid—but really Egypt just does not interest me. I don't know that it interests anyone. The Country is certainly not what I would consider part of the big game plan.

Ayman claims to be interested in literature, but having never seen him with a book in his hand apart from the Qur'an, I find this a little hard to believe. I thought he might have enjoyed reading novels about medicine (Crichton and such like), but he doesn't seem to. Doing my best to make small talk, I once asked him, seeing that he is a doctor, if he ever watched *ER*. He looked at me as if I was a complete idiot and answered, very curtly in my opinion, no.

More fool him. I find the series absolutely riveting and try to watch it every Tuesday evening. Not only is it a very intelligent, thoughtful show, but some of the nurses are quite beautiful. There's a blonde one who is always giving men injections, usually in the ass, and I often picture myself on the receiving end of her needle…

April 12.

Sent Ariel Sharon an email this morning, on the eve of his departure for Washington. The man sees himself as Churchillian, which can't be so hard for him to imagine: he does after all actually look like a British bulldog—or is he more like a Sumo wrestler? I certainly wouldn't trust him as far as I could throw him—and being as wide as he is tall, I couldn't throw him very far.

I wrote: *Dear Shazza, I have it on good authority that Bush is considering con-*
verting to Judaism in order to sew up the Jewish vote in the coming election. A little
nudge from you could get him over the line. Have a safe journey, Osama.

Then I sent a quick email off to George W: *Dear George, Ariel has confessed to*
a mutual acquaintance that he is seriously considering converting to Islam if it will
guarantee him the Prime Ministership of a united Israeli-Palestinian state. He needs
your encouragement. Osama.

Hopefully I have made their little get together more interesting.

April 16.

I'm thinking about buying a refrigerator. We don't really need one: most of the
time it's freezing up here, but they do look great, and it would give me a lot of
status amongst the warlords in these parts. There's one in the latest Walmart catalogue: a 10.5 cubic foot midsize Haier. It's a refrigerator-freezer, but the bit I
really like is, it has a Dispense-a-Can storage space. You take out one can and the
next one rolls into place—just like that. It's very neat.

It's a little upsetting that the catalogue describes this refrigerator as offering
"limited space," and ideal when you "want a smaller, second refrigerator." They
make it sound second best. Perhaps I should go for something bigger—maybe a
two-door upright, the kind that has a freezer on one side and a refrigerator on the
other? That would impress people more. Need to do a bit more online research
before I choose, I think.

April 20.

Photographs of prisoners being tortured at Abu Ghraib prison in Iraq have been
released. Shock, horror around the world. Naked prisoners being piled on top of
each other, prisoners with wires attached to their genitals, prisoners being savaged
by dogs and others being led around on all fours, like dogs. I have also been
informed that many prisoners are being forced to listen to Russell Crowe CDs 24
hours a day, seven days a week. The latter, in particular, I find unbelievably cruel.

However, I can't think why everyone is so surprised by these revelations. It's
what I've always said: the Americans are no better than anyone else—apart, that
is, from being able to sell this holier than thou, self-righteous bullshit. They're
very good at that—and obviously get it from their President, who has to be the
most sanctimonious man on the planet.

They say they want Iraq to be a democracy. What they mean is they want the
country to vote for the American way of life. A country can only be democratic if
it supports America. It makes me crazy, the tortuous way they think.

April 22.

A beautiful spring day. Late in the afternoon I was sitting alone on the mountain-side, watching the sun go down. Thousands of feet below me I could see the sparkling waters of Lake Navar and, to the south-east, the tiny village of Giru. A few miles beyond the lake, but out of sight, lay the main Kabul-Kandahar road.

Some goats were grazing nearby, and I found myself staring at one of them, a rather frisky, naughty looking creature, rather longer than might be considered socially acceptable. It was like one of those romantic TV commercials, all violin music and lenses coated in Vaseline. I came out of my reverie with a start. I was horrified, and actually found myself blushing. Luckily, Abu suddenly appeared out of the cave to come and look for me. What if I had been left alone for another ten minutes...?

It doesn't bear thinking about.

April 29.

I think we must stop playing Monopoly before someone gets killed. They are all such bad losers. We played this evening and again it ended in tears.

Omar, a baby-faced recruit from Saudi Arabia who looks as if he doesn't even shave, is a poor loser. Perhaps this is because he's the youngest in his family and was spoilt. He does the same thing every time he's losing, and yet however hard the rest of us try to stop him performing his little trick, he always manages to catch us unawares. He stands up suddenly and accidentally-on-purpose knocks the board flying. Tokens, money, property cards, Chance and Community Chest cards, hotels and houses all go flying.

"Oops, sorry," he says, "now we don't know who would have won."

"So-and-so was winning," someone usually says at this stage, "so we'll have to say he won."

"No," says Omar indignantly, "that's not right. He might have been winning, but that doesn't mean he would have won. We didn't finish the game, so no one won."

"Don't be stupid, Omar. So-and-so would have won. He was way ahead of everyone else."

"It doesn't matter. We didn't finish the game, so he didn't win. I might have won." By now he is getting more and more agitated.

"No, you wouldn't. You didn't even have any houses."

"But I might have won."

"No, you wouldn't. It would have been impossible for you to win."

At this point Ali will usually pick up his rifle or a knife, in a most off-hand manner, and say very quietly: "Shut up, Omar."

This always works. Omar will sit down, blushing furiously and looking resentful, but at least he shuts up.

Ali is the worst loser of them all. If he doesn't win—which is most of the time thanks to Ayman—he can look very dangerous; dangerously dangerous. He even stands out in this crowd. He sits there in stony silence. Usually he has his headphones over his ears and is listening to *Terrorist* by D.J. Vadim. He barely moves, he simply glowers at everyone. It can be most unsettling. He hasn't attacked any of us yet, but whenever I win a game, I always feel uneasy. I watch him closely and thank Allah that Abu is sitting by my side.

This evening, when Ali landed on Regent Street, where Ayman had a hotel, Ali picked up his Kalashnikov and released the safety catch. You could have heard a pin drop. He pointed it at Ayman. I didn't want to get involved, but I thought he was done for. I'll say one thing for my deputy, however, he wasn't fazed at all. He just smiled and said: "My dear boy, what's £1,275 to a good looking young fellow like yourself?" But I don't think Ali could hear him, anyway, what with his headphones on and the volume turned right up.

Ali raised the Kalashnikov and fired several rounds into the blackness high above our heads, into the roof of the cave. It was deafening, but luckily we were too far underground for the sound to travel to the surface. Everyone immediately leapt off their cushions and remonstrated with Ali, except for Ayman who remained seated and simply smiled at him. I don't believe he even blinked. Then Ali stabbed the point of his dagger into some money, like it was a chunk of bread, and handed it to my deputy.

Compared to the others, I think I'm a pretty good loser. I just get up, go to bed and take a couple of sleeping pills. I think that's more sporting, personally.

Abu is possibly a better loser than me, but that's only because I don't believe he understands the difference between winning and losing, His little brain hasn't quite worked it out yet. He's quite happy just moving his boot token (which he always insists on playing with) around the board and saying, "Let's kick butt, Abs."

May 2.

The latest word from Washington is that at the end of last month Paul Wolfowitz appeared in front of some Senate hearing and got the total number of US soldiers killed in Iraq—a war for which he was largely responsible—wrong by many hundreds. And this from a man who, like most of Bush's gang, has never served himself. It must make the US army feel loved.

May 5.

Georgie Porgie has publicly apologized for the abuse and torture of Iraqi prisoners in Abu Ghraib prison.(He looked very much how I imagine he must have been 30 or 40 years ago apologizing to the Silver Fox for having spilt his milk at table: small and contrite with downcast eyes. "I'm sorry, it was an accident. I didn't mean to do it.") I'm not sure why he bothers. The rest of the world already knows that America is no better than the regime it overthrew. The rumor is, before flying prisoners from Iraq or Afghanistan to Guantanamo Bay in Cuba, they take them to Egypt to torture them. It seems no one's bothered by torture in that Country, so the Americans don't have to worry about human rights protests and such like. I must tell Ayman that about his beloved Egypt; maybe it'll shut him up.

Every night, when I pray at bedtime, I thank Allah for having sent Bush to be my enemy—and Sharon, too. They each have so many opportunities to heal the rifts with Muslims, and every time they turn away from them. Without fail, they keep Muslims dispossessed and in a state of poverty. Without fail, they play into my hands. Without fail, they further my cause. Without fail, they turn their backs on peace.

They are my staunchest allies, and for that I am extremely grateful.

May 6.

Curl up on the floor of the cave with a tub of Michael's Frozen Custard (sealed off by a curtain from the others), and watch the final episode of *Friends.* To be honest, the show has never captivated me, but I watch it because of Courtney Cox. I would be quite happy if she was on TV 24 hours a day, seven days a week all by herself. She wouldn't have to say anything, or do anything, just be there.

May 7.

Karen Hughes has come back into the limelight she loves so much, after two or three years looking after her family. She's flogging her autobiography or something. Not sure if I can be bothered to read it, even though Georgie Porgie seems to believe the sun shines out of one of her orifices. I'm sure he misses her, and will be trying to lure her back to the White House so that he has another strong woman's hand to hold. I think he feels safe if he has Condo holding one hand and Karen the other. So what does that leave Laura to hold onto?

He certainly likes tough women. Is that because he's so weak—or because he was brought up by such a dominating, cold mother? Having Barbara as a Mum would not be an enticing proposition—like trying to get warmth and comfort from an iceberg.

But Georgie still has that awful Karl Rove to lean on, his portly, Machiavellian back-stabber, or—as he prefers to call him—his Turd Blossom.

Turd Blossom: shitkicker extraordinaire.

May 9.

George goes to bed about nine o'clock. It's unbelievable. He's like an old man, in his carpet slippers and with a cup of Ovaltine. I am 48 and still leaping around the mountains, sleeping in caves, and fighting the enemy in hand-to-hand combat. Laura needs a man, not some old granddad. Bet he can't even get it up nowadays. I think the fact that Laura has divulged this information to the Press (the early to bed bit, not the bit about not being able to get it up) is a barely disguised cry for help, the nearest she could come to an outright appeal to me to rescue her. I must not let her down. The poor woman must be so frustrated. Is that the fate of all librarians?

May 11.

Thought for the day:

The *USS Cole*, a giant destroyer, was destroyed by a small dinghy, just as the giant US of A will be destroyed by the small al-Qaeda network. Aphorism of the day.

May 17.

Today I arranged matters so that Samah and I would be left alone in the cave. When she served me tea, I winked at her in a most suggestive manner. She quickly looked away.

"I sent Mohammed off with Abu on a task," I said casually.

"Yes, sir?"

"I thought it would give us the opportunity to talk, Samah." (Talk was the last thing on my mind.) She looked at me, startled. I winked again, putting even more meaning into the wink this time. She busied herself with some dishes.

"I have been feeling very lonely recently." I moved closer to her.

"I'm sorry to hear that, sir."

"Are you, Samah? Do you care?" I stepped towards her. "You have ignored me!" I cried out. I grabbed her, just managing to get a hand on one of her breasts before she twisted free.

"I'm sorry, sir, but I have work to do, the evening meal to prepare." She was flustered, avoiding my eyes.

I was spurned. I cannot understand it. She gave herself to me once, why not again? Had she and Mohammed reached some agreement together? It seemed most unfair to cut me out like that. He is my friend after all.

I went back online and stroked the palm tree myself while viewing *Hot babes of the Kalahari.*

May 20.

The sheer hypocrisy of the man astounds me. He rambles on about the Good Lord every day, and yet he leads a life which would surely make any true Christian curl up and die of embarrassment.

I have to admit I'm not too hot on the Ten Commandments, but I know they say something about not killing people, and Georgie Porgie must be responsible for even more deaths than me—which is really saying something! Certainly, as Governor of Texas he set the record for the highest number of executions by any governor in American history (including a few innocents from what I hear.) And being a staunch supporter of the National Rifle Association ever since he acquired public office would give him a few hundred more notches on his rifle.

Then there have been all the thousands of deaths he has been responsible for in Afghanistan, Iraq, the Balkans, Colombia, Sudan and the Philippines, not to mention all those he's killed at second-hand, in Palestine, through Sharon. Yet no one calls Bush a terrorist. It is most puzzling. I wish I could get my head around it.

The Ten Commandments also mention not coveting things (yet he certainly coveted, and was obsessed by, the power, wealth and prestige that he knew the Presidency would bestow on him.)

They talk about the sanctity of the family, yet he's responsible for breaking up and killing possibly thousands of families in Palestine, Iraq and Afghanistan, and making thousands, probably millions of kids, orphans. Thanks, Daddy!

The Commandments also go on about not committing adultery, yet surely he's done that at some time? Like father, like son as they say, and Dad had a notorious reputation with the ladies from what I've heard.

And about not worshipping false gods, yet he worships at the altar of Mammon, and steals other countries' oil every day. Also, he's rumored to be notching up an enormous fortune for himself in the White House with the help of his big business cronies.

The Commandments go on about loving your neighbor, yet Georgie Porgie was once an out-and-out racist (maybe still is?) having a Confederate flag on the wall of his room at school. And he's a real gay hater (love to know how he reconciles that with Cheney's lesbian daughter, Mary. Maybe that subject is simply ignored. When Cheney walks into the Oval Office: "Hi, Dick, how's Lynne?" "She's real good, thanks, Mr. President." "And Elizabeth, how's she getting along?" "She's good, too, thanks for asking, Mr. President." "Well, then let's get down to it.")

I mean, just how does Georgie get away with it? He's no different to those evangelists in the US, who preach the way of the Lord while accumulating hundreds of millions of dollars for themselves at the same time.

At least I'm honest. I'm no hypocrite. Whereas the once coke snorting, trigger happy, money grubbing Georgie Porgie…Well, you just have to admire the gall of the man. When he eventually fronts up at those pearly gates Christians believe in, St Peter's going to laugh himself silly—possibly becoming quite hysterical before he's able to pull himself together and send the President "down below," to where he surely belongs. For a very long time.

May 23.

Fabulous news. Michael Moore has won the Palme d'Or at the Cannes Film Festival for "Fahrenheit 9/11." And the lucky devil got his award presented to him by Charlize Theron—which, to me, would be a much greater accolade. To hell with the statue, get an invitation back to her room.

George will be pleased. I imagine this great documentary must be compulsory viewing at the White House film evenings—maybe with discussions, and a little soul-searching, afterwards?

May 27.

The UK says it will send more troops to Iraq. They're getting in deeper and deeper. Everyone denies this is going to be another Vietnam. I think they could be in for a surprise.

I wonder what Laura thinks about it all. I imagine her having long arguments with George in bed (no, no, *no!* I try not to think of her in bed with *him!*) But I'm certain she will be doing her best to make him see the error of his ways. I really find it hard to believe that my little leftie librarian can live in the same house as that out-and-out fascist.

June 1.

Today five of us left the Sheikh Hazrat mountain range and traveled the fifty miles to Kandahar by four wheel drive. The Land Cruiser's air conditioning system wasn't working, so it was stifling, even with all the windows open—which meant we were soon coated in a thick layer of dust. Much of the road is little more than a dirt track, with a vertical cliff on one side and a precipitous drop on the other. I prayed we didn't run into anyone coming in the opposite direction—especially with the maniac Ali driving. I don't think anyone's ever told him about the brake: he accelerates even when we are going downhill. I only just managed to stop him as we hurtled through Farm-e Hadda. We had almost passed the few derelict houses on either side of the main street (as well as run over a mangy looking dog, that I'm certain was intentional) when I persuaded him to halt so that we could have coffee with Fatima.

She appeared flustered when she came to the front door and saw me there, but agreed (let's face it, she did not have any option) to accompany me to a small room at the back of the house, while my comrades stayed and chatted to the kids. I was soon reacquainting myself with her hills and valleys.

I feel guilty betraying Laura like that, but I am a man and it is what men do. A man, a real man like myself, has physical needs, and I'm sure she would understand that and forgive me. Ten minutes later we were back on the road to Kandahar. I didn't even get my coffee.

Ali always insists on playing *Terrorist* at full volume on the car's stereo system, but he still managed to turn round from the driver's seat and shout to me, "Cleared your tubes back there, did you, Osama?" He gave me a meaningful grin and a thumbs up, then turned back to the road just in time to stop us from plummeting into a ravine.

I thought it best to ignore him. "I'm praying," was all I said, "please do not speak to me for awhile." I was praying too—that we didn't swerve straight off the road.

"I'd say you've been worshipping at a different temple," he shouted back in a really vulgar way, and guffawed loudly. I could see the other men trying not to laugh.

Kandahar is about the only place on earth I still feel relatively safe. (Two men, probably CIA operatives, did try to assassinate me there in 1997, which really pissed me off, but today the city is still a Taliban stronghold, even though they were ousted from government two years ago.) When I drive into the city, founded by Alexander the Great on Central Asia's most important trade route, I can always feel myself relax. Many people wave to me as I drive past, and I wave back. It makes me feel like the Queen of England. This gave me the idea that maybe I should start making a televised address to the people on Christmas Day, too. Give the old gal a bit of competition. "My deputy and I…" Instead of a corgi, I could have a goat sitting at my feet.

As well as an al-Qaeda board meeting, I had arranged a meeting with the one-eyed devil himself. The board meeting was nothing exceptional. I always allow the others to believe they have some say in what we do, but it is a fiction. Most of them are too dumb to organize an orgy on a sheep farm.

Ayman is the exception; he is too clever by half. It still annoys me that some Westerners think he's cleverer than me, "the brains behind al-Qaeda" is how they frequently put it. I don't believe he's any cleverer than me, I really don't. What brain power he does possess is spent on coming up with new ways to seduce little kids. And that can't be so taxing, surely?

We sat majlis style on cushions in one of my remote houses on the outskirts of the city. There is an old table in the room, a photograph of Mullah Omar on one wall, which, like all the other walls, consists of cracked and chipped mud, and bare floorboards.

The highlight of our get-together was a report from the head of our accounts department, the Sudanese, Abu-al-Hasan. He flew into Kandahar a couple of days ago. It was good to see him again. We embraced warmly.

Our finances are in good shape, he reported. Despite the US and sundry other countries doing their best to shut down our means of support, money is still flowing in: from legitimate business interests in the Sudan and other parts of Africa, and from quite a number of successful extortion rackets in Saudi Arabia.

"Pay up or we'll bomb your business back into the Stone Age," or, "until it fucking looks like the WTC" is how our man on the spot likes to put it to these businessmen.

"Can't you be a bit more subtle," I always ask, "a little less direct?" But I gather he never varies his approach. It obviously works, so I feel I can't complain too much.

To the surprise of all of us, our opium interests in Afghanistan are hugely profitable. Local peasant farmers have been encouraged to increase opium cultivation by more than 5,000 acres over the past year. This encouragement usually takes the form of burning their regular crops. The result is al-Qaeda now has a significant share of Afghanistan's opium and heroin industry, bringing us in at least $US25 million a year.

We briefly discuss other ways of raising revenue. Abu-al-Hasan tells us that he has parted with over $US40 million and a couple of tons of opium trying to persuade the Chechen mafia to obtain some enriched uranium or a nuclear warhead from Russia. As yet we have nothing to show for our investment. I tell him to persevere, and the others nod their agreement.

The best news is the amount of money we're making in Iraq. The Americans are doling out cash there faster than they can print it back in the States, and they're not too careful who they hand it over to. Much of it ends up with our supporters, which means that the Americans are basically financing the war against themselves. How good is that! Of course any of the money that we can't get our hands on is going straight back to American companies, like Halliburton and KBR, in the US, so virtually nothing is reaching the Iraqis themselves.

We went on to discuss Khalid Shaikh Mohammed's confessions. I don't know what they're doing to him, but he certainly seems to be spilling the beans. Luckily, he only knows so much. Ayman asked if I wanted him eradicated before he said anything else, but I thought it was too risky. He would be too well protected. If he was in an Indian jail it would be a different story. You can get someone out of an Indian jail for a few rupees, no questions asked.

"Anyway," I added, "he has probably already told them everything he knows."

My main worry is that he will be handed over to the Americans. At present the ISI(11) is refusing to hand him over. I understand they're worried he would reveal too much about their own dealings with al-Qaeda.

This is an excellent example of why I keep my cards so close to my chest. Even at Board meetings I do not say too much. Apart from myself, the only person who knows all of al-Qaeda's plans is Ayman. Rather than be allowed to fall into the hands of the US, either of us would have to be killed—but I sincerely hope that it won't come to that. Not my cup of tea at all, being killed by one of my followers. I only ever agreed to that plan because I don't expect it to happen.

Today, for example, I did not tell them about our plans for the American election. There are teams in the US who know a part of the plan for the Republican Party Convention in September, but there is only one man in the US who knows all about the plan—and he is kept well back from center stage. He is the puppet master off-stage.

After the Board meeting I went and met with Mullah Omar. As usual, we saw eye to eye on most issues. Ha, ha. I told him I had dropped in on his daughter earlier in the day, but didn't mention fucking her.

June 2.

Hearing about Cannes the other day has set me thinking: I wonder if Hollywood would be interested in making a film of my life. I'm talking an epic, of course, so one would tend to look to Spielberg to direct or, perhaps—if there were no budgetary worries—to Frances Ford Coppola or Michael Cimino, a vastly underrated director in my opinion. Michael Moore would be a more sympathetic director, but I'm not sure he has the scope or the vision.

But the intriguing question is, who would play *moi?* It's such a shame Peter *Lawrence of Arabia* O'Toole is past it—he would have been perfect: stature, sexy voice and visionary, dreamlike air. And he definitely looks good traipsing across sand dunes and spotting mirages on the horizon.

Tom Cruise is certainly a big enough star and crazy enough, but he's a midget. They'd have to have him standing on a box for the whole shoot. Tim Robbins has the height, the almost sympathetic political leanings, he's a great actor, but he is getting a bit paunchy. Could he scale such peaks—and I'm talking both emotional and geographical ones here?

Sean Penn—now he's an interesting possibility. He has the magnetic personality, the athletic physical presence, the feeling of interior depth, he has done plenty of war films (including *The Thin Red Line*), and he would doubtless leap at the opportunity to play such a complex and larger-than-life character as myself.

Then there is the decision about who to put opposite him. Isabelle Huppert, Julia Roberts, Emmanuelle Beart, Helena Bonham Carter, Diane Keaton, Julianne Moore, Michelle Pfeiffer...The list just goes on and on. I'd be happy for any of them to play my various wives. Being the adviser on the film, with my own motor home, it would therefore be necessary for each of these ladies to visit me regularly for instructions and advice on how best to play their part. I could show them what I expect of my wives.

June 3.

The American soldiers are paper tigers. After a few blows in Somalia, they ran in defeat. And it was the same in the first Gulf War. After all the hoopla and media propaganda, after they had destroyed the infrastructure of the Country, and destroyed the baby formula factories and all the factories where civilians found work, and after they had destroyed all the dams and bridges that are needed for the growing of food and the communications between people—after destroying all of that, they fled. They left, dragging their corpses and their shameful defeat behind them.

This defeat pleased me very much, the way it pleases all Muslims.

They will do exactly the same in Iraq, when it becomes too hot for them.

The so-called super powers vanish into thin air when the going gets tough. They do not have the stomach for it. I think the United States is very much weaker than Russia, and look what I did to Russia.

Our brothers in Somalia saw the weakness, frailty and cowardice of the US troops. Only eighty of them were killed, and yet they fled into the heart of darkness, frustrated, after they had caused great commotion about the new world order.

I know that some people blame us for the hundreds of thousands of Sudanese who died in the civil war after the Americans had left, and I admit that was unfortunate.

But in the grand scheme of things, what does it matter if a few people die? A few here, a few there, it's not so important.

June 7.

I'm lucky I have enough time on my hands to write this diary. It's because I don't like to spend too long on the computer, as I sometimes feel twinges of what I suspect could be the onset of RSI.

There is nothing else for me to do, apart from pray, and you can only spend so many hours of the day in prayer. So I write this diary. It could be a valuable document one day—even now. *Inside one of the Great Minds of the 21ˢᵗ Century*, that kind of thing. Leather bound with gold lettering on the spine. I am always amazed that Murdoch has never called me and offered to buy my story. Suppose he's too busy chasing stories from the likes of Posh Spice and trashy American starlets.

June 13.

"I don't want the details," he is said to shout at his advisers. "Just give me the broad picture." The truth is he can't take in anything too complex—do they not realize that? The only part of a newspaper he reads is the sports pages. His brain is too small for anything more. It's stunted, barely formed, like a child's.

Cheney and Rumsfeld probably brief him with little picture books.

"If all the poor people in America are Democrats, Georgie, then what do we do with them? That's right, we take away their medical benefits. See, that's the Red Cross first aid box being taken away from this family in a Chicago slum.

"We also tax them more than the rich, because that will stop them breeding—breeding is another word for having babies, Georgie. See, that man is being slugged by a big tax sledgehammer right now. Ooooh, I bet that hurts! But it's for their own good, isn't it, Georgie? We don't want these poor people to produce more poor people. That would not only be a calamity, it would be a drain on the Country's resources. It would also mean less money for you and I, and we can't have that, can we?

"We must also make sure they don't get any work. See, here's a man wasting his time sleeping above a subway ventilation shaft in Times Square. Not only is he too lazy to work, but there aren't any jobs even if he wanted to.

"Good, well done, Georgie. It's coming along nicely. Soon we'll be able to go onto the next lessons: How to Fix an Election, How to Steal another Man's Oil from Right Beneath his Nose, and How to Lose all your Best Friends around the World."

The President is proud of his stupidity, that's the amazing thing. Most people will run around shouting, Hey, I have an IQ of 156, but he's quite happy running around boasting, Hey, guys, my IQ's only 92!

Now that really is stupid. Duh!

June 16.

The newspapers are carrying an increasing number of articles on the madness of Tony Blair. They mention his Messianic tone of voice, and the way he rolls his eyes when he is talking—or preaching. It is all about his conviction over Iraq, the fact that he and Bush were right to invade the Country.

Conviction politics is not something the West is used to, of course. It makes them feel uneasy, especially the English, who believe it is ungentlemanly to show too much enthusiasm for anything, except perhaps for the weather and corporal punishment. They do like a good spanking, however, and if this can be combined in some way with the rain and the cold, then that is a good thing. Like, "I will give you a good spanking if it rains today. I'll paddle you in the paddock."

The West feels more at ease with the mealy-mouthed utterances that emerge from the likes of that Australian Prime Minister—whose name escapes me right now. Luke warm waffle, pompous twaddle, lips stitched tighter than his backside.

I would be more worried about Tony's mental state, except that is exactly what they used to write about me: Messianic. Maybe we are brothers? There again, maybe he is just nuts. When I think about it, that's the more likely scenario.

June 17.

Pastrami sandwich arrives from the Carnegie Deli with a huge bite taken out of it. And you could have bounced the rye bread off the cave wall it was so stale. The messenger (some dirty, stinking peasant) denied he was the culprit, but it matched his bite pattern, so I slit his throat. Made me feel a bit like Marie *Let them Eat Cake* Antoinette, but I'm not going to lose sleep, or my head, over that. Underlings have to learn their place in the great scheme of things.

June 19.

Abu has confessed to me that his dream is to own a gym. "I want all that equipment, boss. You know, the shiny barbells and dumbbells, the benches and treadmills. I've read about them. They have mirrors round the walls so you can see yourself while you're exercising."

"Why do you want to see yourself while you're exercising?" I was intrigued—and suspicious. I suspected it might be for the same reason people have mirrors on the bedroom ceiling.

"I don't know, boss. I guess it's so that you can see your muscles growing." So, yes, it was like a bedroom ceiling mirror. "You can watch your abs develop, study your pecs and lats, that kind of thing."

I was none the wiser, but I was happy to let him have his dream.

"I'd have loud music playing all day, the kind that makes you want to sweat, pump those muscles, push yourself that little extra bit. You need music to get people's adrenalin going, boss."

He set me thinking about all those hot young women in their skimpy lycra leotards, high cut over the hips and low cut across the breasts. I could see their sculpted bodies bending over, reaching up, swiveling this way and that, pumping, pumping, pumping, their muscles taut, the sweat glistening between their—oh, but I was bringing myself out in a sweat just thinking about them.

I'm sure Abu's mind (if it can be called such a thing) was working along the same tracks, but I refrained from asking him. He had a faint smile on his face while he was telling me all this, as if he could see his gym right there in front of him (although it may have been the women he was grinning at.)

I felt sorry for him that his dream was so distant, but only momentarily. He is no different to a dog dreaming of a bone. He is quite happy with his dream, and it is possible that the dream is even better than the reality.

I have seen him doing press-ups (over a hundred at a time) and sit-ups on the floor of the cave, in the dirt, and he is content. He makes do with what he has to hand. But I still felt it was in order for me to remind him of why he is here. "Concentrate on killing the infidel for now, Abu, then one day you will have your dream. In Mecca or Medina—or maybe you will go back home to Algeria."

"I know, boss. I don't forget that, it's just nice to dream a little sometimes."

June 22.

Drank far too much last night. Became quite melancholy and made the mistake of calling the White House. Asked to speak to Laura—said I was a personal friend—but, after a lot of toing-and-froing between various secretaries, switchboards and personal assistants, suddenly found George W. on the end of the line. "I don't want to speak to you," I slurred, "want to speak to your wife."

"Mercy me, is that you, Osama?"

"Maybe."

"Are you plum crazy calling this time of night?"

"Wanna speak to Laura."

"That's about as likely as grass growing around a hog trough, Osama. You know that."

"Wanna speak to Laura," I shouted down the phone. "Wanna speak to Laura!"

"Now don't get your cows running. She's asleep right now, and so was I until you called. It's not a good time to tell you the truth."

I took another mouthful of whisky, trying to give my concentration a bit of a boost. I had to bite the bullet. "George, there's something you should know." I spoke slowly, trying to enunciate every word. "Got to tell you the truth about Laura and me. You've got to try and understand."

"Laura and you? Yeah?" He sounded surprised. I thought he'd have suspected something by now, but maybe not. He wasn't too quick, that's for sure.

"I'm in love with your wife, George. I love Laura."

There was deafening silence. "George? You still there, George?"

Finally, he said: "You think the sun comes up just to hear you crow, don't you, Osama?"

"Now don't get mad on me, George. These things happen, you know. Love makes one powerless. There's not much a man can do about it. Stupid if you take it personally. You know what? I think it's because she's bored living in Washington all the time, visiting libraries and opening fetes. A woman needs more than that, George. A woman needs some excitement in her life, a bit of romancing, adventure, and a man who can stay up a little later than nine o'clock. Know what I mean, George?"

"You're lower than a snake's belly, Osama, and I tell you what, I feel meaner than a junkyard dog. So I suggest you get back to your cave, or wherever it is you hang out, and you put these stupid notions out of your mind. Your sort don't rightly belong on the same planet as my little lady. G'day to you." And he cut me off. Just like that.

I'm not ashamed to admit it, I had a little cry and drank another glass of whisky. I had to figure out how to speak to Laura direct. I'm sure she feels the same way as me, I just need to talk to her.

June 23.

Some evenings I will go through my press cuttings. I did it again this evening because there was nothing worth watching on TV. I hate the way they put on all the rubbish programs during summer, as if everyone is away on holiday, at the beach or in the garden. What am I supposed to be doing, I ask myself: having a barbecue on a nearby mountainside, followed by a game of baseball or cricket? "Why not invite those nice Americans who have moved in next door over for a drink?" Give me a break.

I keep my cuttings in large books with different colored pages. I have one for each year—although there are three for 2001. Each newspaper cutting has a little caption, with the name of the publication and the date it appeared. I write these in myself. I have quite a library now—as well as videos of my public appearances.

I have heard that American Presidents do the same. It often seems to me that the only reason they seek the Presidency is so they can justify their actions later. They keep all their speeches and press cuttings, video tapes of their TV appearances and then, when they leave the White House, they collect all of these memorabilia together and place them in a library. It's an attempt to set their place in history. It's not such a bad idea really.

Even though I am loathe to copy anything the Americans do, I am thinking seriously of building an Osama bin Laden Library. I have made some preliminary sketches. At the moment it looks like a fusion of the Parthenon and the Reichstag, with a passing obeisance to the new Hong Kong international airport. I am thinking on the grand scale: statues of thinkers and philosophers, of Karl Marx, Stalin and people like that, plus many, many statues of myself scattered throughout the extensive gardens. Also a museum, with my letters and diaries, my childhood toys, including my game of Monopoly, my university degree, my old clothes, an empty yoghurt carton with my name on it, makeshift bombs, my Kalashnikov and so on and so forth. There would be desks for those who wish to study, and moving, push button exhibits for the children.

The library could be in Kandahar, I suppose, or even Kabul once the Taliban get back in power. But the place I would really like to build it is in Saudi Arabia. Next to the mosque in Medina or in Mecca would be ideal. I could catch the pilgrims after they have been to the mosque, possibly even make it an officially recognized part of the Hajj.

Once the Americans and the corrupt Royal Family have been thrown out of the country, I am sure my family would quickly realize the benefits of welcoming me home and would be happy to construct such a library for me. I could probably get them to do it for cost.

My big plan is to ask Laura to come and open the library for me. I believe she would regard this as a singular honor. When I become caliph, I'm sure she'll be more than happy to acknowledge me. But she would have to come without her husband. I'm not having him at the opening. After all, if he stayed at home clearing the brush from around his ranch or whatever it is he does, it would be the perfect opportunity to woo Laura.

"Would you like to come upstairs and see my manuscripts?"

June 28.

I'll say one thing for the man, he has a sense of humor. They say he was a real practical joker in his youth—you know, the kind of high jinks that really hurt other people's feelings, but if they didn't laugh it was because they "didn't have a goddam sense of humor." Today he had me in stitches—he had all of us in stitches: he, or the US, handed power back to the Iraqis. Oh yes!

- So why are you still in our Country?

- Because you're not yet ready to run it yourselves.

- So why is your army still here?

- Because you're not in a position to control your people.

- But why are you still killing our countrymen?

- Because we think there's an outside possibility they're insurgents.

- But is that an excuse for still taking all our oil?

- We only do that because you have to pay us for invading your Country in the first place.

- So why are you still desecrating our religious places?

- Not being religious, we don't give a fuck about those.

- But is that an excuse for imprisoning and torturing our people?

- Yes, because they're trying to make us leave your Country.

- So why are you still here if no one wants you here?

- Because we happen to like it here. We can make a lot of money in your Country. Invasion is a profitable business.

July 1.

We were arguing about the Euro 2004 Final between Greece and Portugal. None of us can quite believe that two such useless teams have beaten the best in the world and are now to meet in the Final. I'm not certain I shall even bother to watch the game.

As I said to Abu, we would have bombed the ground if we'd known two boring teams like that were going to end up playing each other. We were expecting Italy, Germany or even, heaven forbid, England. Certainly not Greece or Portugal. But it's too late to organize anything now. More's the pity.

July 10.

Mullah Omar's brother-in-law has been captured by Afghan security forces. It is a blow, not because he has anything to do with the Taliban—or only in a very minor way—but because the two men are very close. It is a blow for my friend.

July 15.

Last night Laura and I plotted how she could best leave George. She does not want to upset him, but feels she can no longer stay with him. She said it was because he was becoming increasingly "bombastic"—that was the word she used: "bombastic." I said to her, "You mean, fanatical?" She smiled sadly, but did not answer. She is too upset to talk about it much.

"I think he is out of his depth," I said. "He is not a great man, but he is living through a time of great events. He is being pushed to his limits." I wanted her to take out of this that I, on the other hand, was a great man, but I'm unsure as to whether or not she made this connection. "He's a little man—a tall little man, if you know what I mean."

I think more than half the reason she is desperate to leave him is because she wants to come and live with me in the mountains. She is just too shy to come out and say it. I took her in my arms (I could see where this was going!), but then woke up.

It was Abu's stentorian snoring that woke me. I was so disappointed, I kicked him. He rolled over. He stopped snoring, but no matter how hard I tried I was unable to get back to the moment when Laura and I had been so rudely interrupted—just before the rude bit. It was very frustrating. I am no fool: I know very well that it is a small step from consoling a woman to doing the business with her.

July 16.

"Our Beloved Leader" on the phone from Pyongyang. He's extremely happy to be a part of the Axis of Evil. I tell him that I believe it is a great honor to receive such a label from the US. He confirms what he told the whole world recently, that his country's nuclear program is military-oriented. When I ask him to help me out with some nuclear know-how, however, he becomes all evasive, saying things like, "Osama, we're a little short of fuel rods right now," or, "We're running low on nuclear weapons at the moment—we only have five in stock." He sounds like he's running a corner store.

"Kim Jong," I said, "you're flogging all your nuclear know-how to everyone else in the world—Iran, Syria and Iraq—so why not to me?"

He was quite blunt: "Osama, I do not trust you. You are friends with no one, not even with North Korea."

I argued with him, saying this was untrue. I told him I was a great admirer of his, and possibly his best friend (to my knowledge he has none at all), but he would not waver. Imagine me being considered more devious than him! I'm not sure if I should be flattered.

He is like the mouse that roared. Certainly he is most adept at leading everyone a merry dance: the Russians, Chinese and Americans. The fat little man is out-maneuvering all of them. He has them bending over backwards to give him anything, anything at all, if he will only drop his nuclear power ambitions.

I sometimes wish I was the head of a country, instead of hiding in these caves. As head of State you have so much more power—as well as many more options.

July 20.

I do not understand why Muslims around the world are not rising up and joining me in the battle against the infidel. There is so much injustice to fight against: Palestine and Iraq, as well as the corrupt regimes of Saudi Arabia, Egypt, Morocco and Indonesia. And yet no one does anything. It worries me this lack of action, this indifference, although I do not say anything to the others. I do not want them to see me as weak.

July 24.

I never thought I'd see the day when I was grateful to the western press, but thanks to a leak by US security forces to the *New York Times,* the newspaper published a story about the arrest of Mahammad Naeem Noor Khan, one of our computer geeks.

After he was arrested a month ago, he agreed to help the security forces in a sting operation to track down al-Qaeda forces around the world. Many of our operatives reported in by email when asked to do so by Noor Khan, and so gave themselves away to the security forces.

Of course, once the *New York Times* had blown their cover, the Pakistan and British security forces were livid, and berated the US in no uncertain terms. They were claiming that they had even had expectations of trapping me. That made me laugh!

They still arrested fourteen of our men in the UK thanks to Khan. They've put him in a safe house somewhere, but we'll still try and eradicate him before he can do any more harm.

August 1.

Have just finished reading Clinton's memoirs. Selective memoirs I would call them. There were no titillating details about Monica Lewinsky, for example. This was very disappointing. She was the only reason I bought the book. I wanted to know how good she was, what technique she used, and whether or not she found any relief for herself. So far as I know, this is never mentioned. We know about her dresses, but did she leave stains all over his suits?

I can't believe he received a million dollars for this rubbish. It's about as revealing as a burka. When people recall Clinton's presidency, they will inevitably link it to Lewinsky: she was the one who brought him down. (She went down on him and brought him down!) So how can he almost completely ignore the subject?

There are only eleven mentions of me in the Index—just eleven!—and of course he makes all the usual excuses for not having killed or captured me. Post justification, I believe they call it.

Anyway, it has made up my mind for me: I have now decided to write my autobiography. Imagine how much I could get! Probably twice as much as Clinton got. But then I told myself that if I wait a few years, during which time I will hopefully become more notorious and therefore more marketable, I could get even more money. The only trouble is I might be bumped off before then, so perhaps I had better do it now? What a difficult decision. I certainly don't want to depart this world and let some stranger make a fortune out of writing about my life—I want it for myself! These diaries will certainly be an invaluable resource for me when it comes down to the writing.

My main worry is that I haven't had enough sexual experiences, because that's what the public wants to read about. I could exaggerate of course, pretend that Samah and I are still doing it. And then there were the women in Lebanon, I could build them up. Maybe I should borrow a bit from Ayman and Ali, and throw in a few boys and some sheep? That would certainly sell my autobiography. Call it *The Goat Fucker of Afghanistan*. That would top the *New York Review of Books'* best sellers list straight away.

August 11.

This evening I phoned one of our operatives in the States from a call box in Sheydan Chowk, the main roundabout in central Kandahar. Even at 11pm there were plenty of people around. I allowed the others to crowd into the phone booth, too, but only on condition they kept really quiet. I had arranged things with the operative the day before—by email. We use the most basic of code words; that's part of the game.

"The Eagle is in Washington this weekend?"

"Yes."

"It is time his wings were plucked," I said slowly and emphatically. Sa'eed started to giggle, but Aymed dug him sharply in the ribs with his elbow, which shut him up.

"Allah be praised, I believe it is so."

"The sands of Arabia run deep."

Back came the reply: "And it takes many stones to build a pyramid."

I waited a moment, then said:

"And has the package been delivered?"

"It will be delivered on Sunday."

Mohammed gave me a big thumbs up.

"To the right address?" I asked.

"To the tourist site in San Francisco, as was agreed," replied the operative.

"It is so. Allah be praised."

Then I rang off. We were all laughing hysterically as we danced and skipped our way back down the quiet, dark street to where we were staying. Almost immediately—certainly by the time we were back in the mountains the next day—the terrorist danger meter in the US would be turned up to maximum, every secret service agent would be running around like a headless chicken, and all of the President's appointments would be cancelled.

"It's great," I said to the men. "One phone call and—bingo!—absolute chaos ensues. Why do we bother with bombs?"

"Oh, but bombs are fun, too, boss," said Mohammed.

Walking back down the street, past the low concrete buildings with their arched, wooden shuttered windows and corrugated iron roofs, we passed a half dozen drunken Special Armed Forces men. We kept our heads down, but muttered "Good evening!" as we passed by, and they were all shouting, "Hi, Mohammed. Wanna drink? Where's your sister? Just been round to see your mother," and other such friendly, heart-warming comments.

When we got back to camp and Ayman heard what we had done, he accused me of being childish. I think he has lost touch with his inner child, that's all. He no longer knows how to enjoy himself. He is all intellect.

August 13.

They're running commercials in the US attacking Kerry's war record in Vietnam. Someone has dug up all these old vets who claim the Democrat leader was either a coward or not as heroic as he likes to make out, never went near any of the fighting, criticized the US for being in Vietnam in the first place, and so on and so forth.

The campaign has all the hallmarks of Rove. In other words, it's all a massive lie, told again and again, until eventually people begin to wonder if it might indeed be true. The most amazing part of it all is that the campaign is running on behalf of, or in support of, a President who was either hiding under his duvet during the entire Vietnam War or tucked safely behind the formidable Barbara's petticoats.

August 14.

Cherie is a mother, wife (which I am willing to overlook for the moment), barrister, chat-show guest, charity worker (that could be my in: I could invite her to raise funds for victims of the Russian occupation of Afghanistan or something equally ridiculous), and now she is an author.

She has written a book about Prime Ministers' wives. It's called *The Goldfish Bowl* and is out in September. I must put in an advance order to Amazon. Maybe I could get a signed copy. *To Osama, with love and respect, Cherie.*

If the book turns out to be any good (and knowing what I do about the woman, I suspect it will be), I might consider asking her to write my biography—the official version. I could still write my autobiography a few years down the track.

I would give her access to my diaries and to my press cuttings file, even grant her several interviews. Who knows where that could lead? In fact, if she read the entries about herself in this diary, she would discover how I felt about her. She would doubtless be moved by such loyal devotion, and possibly soften towards me; yield to my protestations of love. There again, in future, maybe I should cut out all references to my palm tree when I'm writing about her. It might make her blush. Also, I should delete all references to Laura. That could cause a real cat-fight. These women can get terribly jealous, especially when it comes to a spunk like myself.

August 16.

Georgie Porgie and I are fighting on the same side, and until now I have never realized it. Yesterday he said: "Our enemies are innovative and resourceful, and so are we. They never stop thinking about new ways to harm our country and our people, and neither do we."

What would I do without the man? I am growing quite fond of him. In the same way that one would be fond of a mentally handicapped younger sibling.

August 18.

The Olympics are in full swing.

A few months ago I was told of a plan by some of our operatives in Europe to prepare a big "event" at Athens. It was supposed to happen in the main arena during the opening ceremony. I put a stop to it immediately. I put my foot right down and absolutely forbade it.

I didn't tell anyone why. They probably wouldn't have understood if I'd told them I wanted to watch many of the events. I was especially keen to see Ian Thorpe. "Thorpy", or the human torpedo as I believe he is affectionately known, is a phenomenon. Two days into the Olympics, he has already won two gold medals and a silver. The 200 meters was a really exciting race.

I am so pleased Thorpe beat Michael Phelps. I don't really care who beats the Americans, so long as someone does. But they are already second on the medals ladder, behind China, and will almost certainly go on to win. It's only because they have so much money for training their athletes and because they stuff them full of drugs. Anyone could win if they cheat like that. If they played fair, they wouldn't be any better than anyone else.

I have to watch all events with the sound turned right down, of course, so that the others can't hear, but I am still on the edge of my seat. Once, and it may have been when Thorpey won the 200 meters, I let out a shout of delight, shouting "Yes!" and I was suddenly aware of a silence from the rest of the cave. I was wondering what to do, when someone asked: "Are you all right, Osama?"

"Oh yes, thanks," I replied. "Just some good news from one of our operatives in Europe," I lied. But it was a close thing.

When I rejoin the others after watching an Olympic event, when I have to pretend I have been working, it can be a great effort to look calm and collected, and not to let one's excitement betray one.

But today I took delivery of a brand new pair of headphones that I had ordered from overseas. Now I can listen to the commentary turned up loud. This will make the events much more exciting.

Other events I'm looking forward to are the 1,500 meters swimming, the 5,000 and 10,000 meters running (I love the tactics involved in these races), and the finals of the synchronized swimming.

I am just so pleased that I cancelled al-Qaeda's Olympic event. It would have been really disappointing to miss out on this great sporting occasion. Anyway, blowing up the Democratic or Republican Party Conventions will be much more worthwhile, and grab just as many headlines. It will also be more popular with the masses. Unlike the Olympics, most people find the Party Conventions in the US very boring to watch—although equally partisan.

August 20

Our plan to assassinate the Pakistani Prime Minister and other government ministers, and also bomb the US embassy in Karachi, on Pakistan's Independence Day, on the 14th, has failed. Many al-Qaeda operatives have been arrested.

Things haven't been going right recently. I have too many incompetents working for me. I need a success!

August 23.

I had a dream.

I'm given a green card, so Laura and I settle in a small place in the backwoods of California, right on the edge of the Mojave Desert, mountains rising high in the distance, the perfect balance between the environments of Saudi Arabia and Afghanistan. I clear old scrub from around the homestead and breed horses, while she bakes cookies and cleans the house with Clorox. Weekends we go into town in our beat up old station wagon, catch up with the local gossip and buy our provisions for the week. It's a good life.

August 29.

Hicham El Guerrouj has won both the 1,500 and 5,000 meter races. He knelt on the track and wept, thanking Allah for his gift. I'm sure it wasn't lost on the Americans that they had lost to a Muslim.

August 30.

In a joint operation with our Mujahideen brothers, al-Qaeda operatives blew up a truck bomb in the center of Kabul, killing seven.

The only problem is, the Country is in such chaos, I don't suppose anyone really noticed.

September 1.

Just watched *Team America*. Brilliant! I have never laughed so much in my life. Especially liked the bit when Gary is making love to Lisa (some interesting positions there), and when Gary throws up and throws up and throws up outside the bar.

September 4.

We failed to bomb the Republican Party Convention in New York, but then they spent over $US60 million keeping us out, so I'm not sure that it can really be described as a failure. Anyway, I really want Bush to win the election, so it's maybe just as well.

I shall send him a Good Luck card nearer the time. I have instructed all our followers in the US who are eligible to vote to support him. And I'm encouraged that the Party has Jeb working for us (well, "organizing" the count) in Florida. Once again, it could all hinge on that State come November, and we already know what a great job the Governor does in the count-rigging area.

September 8.

Looks like Karl Rove may be behind the leak about Valerie Plame being a CIA operative. There's certainly a stench coming from the White House and Georgie Porgie, as usual, is busy waving his arms around trying to pretend there's no smell anywhere. "He who denied it, supplied it," as my nanny used to say.

September 15.

Ayman has released his own video. He persuaded Omar to operate the camera and together they snuck off one afternoon when no one was around. I confronted him, but he tried to make light of it, saying he thought I was too busy, that it was important to get something out there in the West, and lies like that.

"You don't release videos without my permission," I said.

"Is that right, Osama?" he sneered, and he started clearing his glasses with that filthy handkerchief of his. He was so cool, I was furious. I just know he's after the Number One spot. He is truly desperate to get rid of me. I shall have to watch him.

September 18.

Howard has been re-elected in Australia. Like being voted Chief Lifeguard, in charge of barbies, boogie boarding and babes in bikinis. Ho-hum.... Not to be taken seriously—certainly not as seriously as he takes himself.

September 21.

In today's wars there are no morals. Americans steal our wealth, our resources and our oil. Our religion is under attack. They kill and murder our brothers. They compromise our honor and our dignity and dare we utter a single word of protest against these injustices, we are called terrorists.

September 24.

We had chops this evening, a rare delicacy for us. (Lamb, of course, not pork.)

I said to Ayman, possibly, I admit, a little too quickly: "Do you want both of your chops, Doc?" I was intending to ask everyone in turn around the table, it just happened that he was the first. I believe I asked the question most politely, but he was certainly quick to take it the wrong way.

"Osama, I have only just commenced eating," he snapped back at me. "I have taken only one mouthful of my first chop. I have not yet even had a moment to consider my second chop." He glared at me in a most unsettling way. His eyes became like little slits.

"I thought maybe you were trying to lose weight." (He is, as I believe I have written in my diary before, verging on the plump. He certainly needs to lose some weight.)

"You're most considerate."

I think I detected a hint of sarcasm in his voice.

"I do appreciate you have only just started to eat, please don't think otherwise, but I thought I would get in early, before anyone else asked you. That is all, Doc. I did not want to pressure you. That was certainly not my intention. It is just that if—and I stress the word, if—*if* you do not wish to eat both of your chops, then I would be more than happy to eat one of them for you. Should, however, you wish to eat both, feel free to do so. That is all."

And without even bothering to answer me, he astonished me by stabbing the offending chop with his knife and almost throwing it onto my plate. I don't understand why he gets on his high horse like that. It is quite unnecessary, and simply causes bad feeling. I asked him a simple question, and he goes completely over the top. Orthodox psychopathic behavior, I suppose. For a psychiatrist, I really do think he needs his head examined.

The rest of the meal passed in a strained silence. I wish he would make an effort to be more considerate of others, of our feelings. I managed to sneak a Valium into my mouth without the others seeing, and soon felt calmer.

(I think, one day, when people read these diaries—they are written for posterity, after all—they will be astonished that such a great man as myself has the time to *lower himself* to writing about petty squabbles at the dining table. But the fact is, even the mightiest in the land must, at times, preoccupy themselves with such mundane matters—they are the stuff of living, after all.)

September 28.

I am standing on a sand dune and Georgie Porgie is striding towards me with that Texan swagger of his, all cowboy boots and Stetson. He has entered an area of quick sands and he's slowly sinking. I call out to encourage him to keep walking towards me, and he does so, sinking further and further into the sand. I can't believe my good fortune. Any minute I expect him to realize that he has fallen into quick sands, and to turn away from me and attempt to get back to where the ground is firm, but to my surprise he never does.

He continues to struggle in my direction. Now he is up to his shoulders and I can see only his arms waving in the air, and his head, his chin lifted defiantly skywards. He looks a little surprised. I wave to him as he disappears beneath the sand. His Stetson is all that is left, floating on the surface. But this is the strange part of the dream: when I am left alone, I start to cry. I miss him, I truly miss him!

I always feel my dreams are very portentous, certainly more significant than the dreams of ordinary people. And I believe this is an excellent example of perhaps why I feel this way.

October 1.

We're in a cave near the summit above Gwal Bagh, at around 8,000 feet. It's bitterly cold. The wind's shrieking outside. I'm sitting on the floor of the cave, knees up to my chest, and finding it difficult to write because I'm wearing gloves.

There are only the very basics in the cave. It was never intended to be anything more than an emergency hideout. There are enough blankets for two people, but there are six of us. We have some candles and some packets of biscuits, but no more. We daren't light a fire in case the Americans are still around. We snuggle together for warmth, but however hard I try I am unable to end up against Samah: she's always at least one body away. I think she and Mohammed are plotting to keep us apart.

We were lucky to make it to the cave before dark. If we had been caught out in the open in this weather I think we'd have perished from the cold during the night.

They came just before sunset, to one of the command bunkers. I don't believe we were betrayed; rather I think they stumbled on us by mistake. I'm furious with Khan. He should have given us warning that they were around. I pay him enough to keep an eye open for us, and this is how he treats us. Unless he has a very good excuse, I think I'll have him assassinated and get someone more reliable in his place, someone we can trust.

I shall write down what happened.

It was a typical afternoon. All our afternoons are the same, as are all our mornings. They never vary from one day to the next. Monotony and boredom seem to be my lot in life right now. No wonder I spend my days fantasizing about Laura. Or Cherie. Or Samah. Or anyone at all. I crave excitement.

I was actually on my computer, keeping in contact with overseas brothers and moving some currency around. Omar and Ali were sitting on the floor of the command center at Gwal Bagh chatting about their usual topic of conversation: soccer. (Ali supports Manchester United, while Omar is a Real Madrid man, so discussions are often lively.) Abu was sitting by himself doing nothing, which is what he usually does if he isn't cleaning his rifle or exercising. (I have never known a human being so content to sit and do nothing. He's like an animal in that respect—possibly in many respects.) Samah was with us, too. She was preparing the evening meal, while her husband was at the entrance to the cave, keeping watch.

Fortunately, Samah was only preparing the ingredients for our food at that stage. She hadn't started to cook, so there was no fire lit. Also we had only two lamps lit. One was next to me so that I could see the computer screen, and the other was next to Samah.

Suddenly I was aware of a commotion behind me. I turned. Mohammed had run from the cave entrance and was now dragging Samah towards the back of the cave. For the briefest of moments I thought he had been overcome by the basic animal urge to propagate. I could see his wife's eyes above her hijab, wide with alarm (maybe she thought the same.) But Ali, Omar and Abu had also scrambled to their feet, so I didn't think my initial suspicions could be right, unless they were planning an orgy. Abu was already kneeling on one knee, facing the cave entrance, his rifle propped against his side while he slung bandanas of bullets around his shoulders.

I immediately guessed what was happening, possibly helped by the fact Mohammed had whispered in a low, urgent whisper: "Infidels!" I closed my laptop, and thrust it into my saddle-bag along with my diary. I turned off the lamp, and went and stood close behind Samah. As she was a woman and therefore the least valuable member of our small community, and as I was the most valuable, it seemed the sensible place to position myself. Mohammed and Ali were collecting essential items and feverishly stuffing them into saddle-bags. We had rehearsed this scenario many times before, deciding what had to be taken in the event of an emergency and what could be safely left behind.

The command center we were in yesterday, like several others in the mountains, had a front and a back entrance. It had not been possible to create two entrances for every cave, but where it had been feasible to blast out an escape route from the rear of the cave, we had done so. That all happened around fifteen years ago, in the late Eighties. Praise be to Allah, we were now in such a cave. Most surely he was looking over us yesterday. If it had not been so, it is unlikely I would be writing this now.

Obviously we did not wish to leave the cave—by any entrance—unless it was absolutely necessary. Even though the entrances were quite a distance apart, there was the possibility the Americans had both covered.

Ali, Mohammed and Abu joined us at the back of the cave. We crouched there in the darkness. We could not see the front entrance: it was over a hundred yards away, and the passageway between it and the cave proper was on a gentle rise. The entrance was probably twelve feet above the floor of the cave.

Then we heard voices. We heard them a long time before we saw their owners. I prayed to Allah that we would not be discovered.

We saw the soldiers' legs first as they approached down the slope of the passageway. There were two of them. They weren't in a hurry. One of them was talking, and one was listening to his Walkman. He was playing 50 Cents' *In the Club*. I could hear it quite clearly. I like that song, and I know most of the words. I've seen the video release too, with all those hot women dancing. (Come to think of it, that's probably why I like the song.)

When the two soldiers got to the foot of the passage and reached the cave proper, I could make out that they were both black. Oppressed like us Muslims, I thought, and felt an immediate affinity with them. But this affinity wasn't to last long.

Both men had torches and they were pointing them nonchalantly around the cave. One of them was saying, "If that mother-fucker says that to me one more time, I think I'll blow his fucking head off. I don't give a fuck if he's an officer, I'll fucking blow him away." The soldier listening to music was just nodding. Then one of their beams swept across us as we huddled in the far corner of the cave. Almost immediately the beam swung back again.

"Shit!" one of them cried out (I think it was the one who'd been complaining about his officer.) At that point all hell broke loose. I think it was Abu who fired first. The noise was deafening. In the confines of the cave, the gunfire echoed off every surface. One of the soldiers fell (I don't know if he was dead, or just wounded) and the other dived back into the passageway, hidden by an outcrop of rock. I pressed in closer behind Samah, and prayed. I also quickly squeezed her breasts, knowing that this might be my last chance in this life. She was too stunned to remove my hands. I think she may even have been grateful for the comfort I was giving her. A few seconds later, one of the soldiers lobbed a grenade towards us, but it exploded in the middle of the cave with little effect—apart from the fact I had to let go of Samah's breasts.

"Go!" shouted Abu, and I for one did not need any further encouragement. Using Samah's shoulders, I levered myself to my feet. Abu was firing towards the passageway, keeping the Americans pinned down, while we retreated towards the back exit. We had rehearsed this before. Ali would cover our retreat and, once we had made good our escape, would try to join us. Whether he would be able to was never discussed in any great detail.

We stumbled along the passageway in the dark, Mohammed leading the way, followed by myself, Samah and Omar, with Abu bringing up the rear. We didn't know how much time we had. I was already gasping for breath. I turned round and thrust my saddlebag at Samah, telling her to carry it.

What saved us was the training of the Americans: retreat out of harm's way until reinforcements arrive. We had all expected the soldiers' colleagues to storm down the passageway from the main entrance to the cave, throwing stun grenades or worse, and firing their automatic rifles with complete abandon. However, what transpired, we later discovered, was that the Americans had decided to remain safely on the surface, possibly joined by the two soldiers we'd seen (we never discovered if that was so), and had called in air support. They thought we couldn't escape.

Half an hour later Hawk helicopters had dropped every bomb known to man, including those that could penetrate hundreds of yards through solid rock, onto the cave, completely obliterating it. "They're dropping their million dollar bombs on an empty cave," I kept thinking.

By that time we had reached the col overlooking the next valley, and Ali had joined us. He was positively glowing after his skirmish with the Americans. Even though it was blowing a gale we still felt the explosions. The ground shook, it was like an earthquake. I imagined being buried under many tons of rock. It made me feel sick. I also felt sick about losing one of our command centers—the first we'd lost to the Americans since they arrived here in 2001.

What interests me about the American tactics—if they have any tactics—is this: they'll never know if they've killed me the way they're carrying on. If I had still been in the command center, I would have been buried under an avalanche of rock, and it would have been impossible to ever dig me out to prove that I was dead. Maybe they don't care—which I find a little upsetting. I certainly care.

Ayman and I have planned for such an eventuality. We've made, I think, about four videos that are not time specific: they do not refer to any particular events. They could be released after my death, if my body is never found, and no one will be any the wiser. For all they know, I will still be alive and fighting.

How's that for immortality.

Tomorrow we are heading—if we survive the night—north-east towards Kherezi.

October 3.

Karl Machiavelli Rove has done it again. "Compassionate conservatism." How does he do it? A gem, and quite, quite meaningless—which makes it absolutely brilliant. It will appeal to everyone—well, everyone who hasn't got as brain in his head—and that adds up to an awful lot of people in the States.

I wonder if he would come and work for me? If I paid him enough, I'm sure he would. He'd go and work for the devil himself if there was enough money in it ("You want to sell your soul, Mr. Rove?" "Sorry, Luce, I've already sold it.")

Of course, the fact I don't have any opposition means he'd be wasted with me—although I could use him to dig up some dirt on Bushy. I'm sure he has plenty of stories there!

October 8.

Our drug sidelines are doing well. No sooner do I withdraw all the money from our accounts in Kabul and deposit it overseas (the US is a particularly strong market that I am favoring right now), than they fill up again. Ayman sometimes turns up his nose because we own poppy farms, but I tell him he's being far too sensitive.

"We're gnawing away at the foundations of a corrupt society," I tell him, "undermining its very structure. Every smack head in New York is doing his or her bit for al-Qaeda, helping keep us in business." I was inspired: "Every time one of them shoots up, our glorious campaign moves forward."

"That's fine, Osama, but what about the addicts in Muslim countries? What about the misery we cause amongst our own people?"

"All of our poppy exports go overseas to the West."

"How can you be so sure?"

I waved a hand dismissively. "Don't worry so much, Ayman. Believe me, this drug money is what's keeping us going right now. The Americans have closed down so many of our other sources of revenue, be thankful that we still have this one."

He shook his head, still frowning. I could tell he wasn't happy, but then why should I worry. What did he know?

"The West is exporting their corrosive culture to Islamic countries," I said to him. "And now we are exporting something back that corrodes their society. Their society is as wicked as their culture. It is a good thing, believe me."

October 15.

Today I was walking with Abu to another command bunker. We camped out last night, which can still be a pleasant enough experience at this time of year. On average I move every two to three days, always trying to keep one step ahead of the accursed infidels. Two others were about an hour ahead of us on the same path. We always travel in small, inconspicuous parties of two or three people to avoid drawing attention to ourselves, and to avoid being seen by the ever-present predator drones that circle above these mountains day and night. We can contact each other by radio in the event of an emergency.

It was a beautiful morning. The sun was shining for the first time in days, and I was feeling at peace with the world. Even the pain in my right hip has disappeared, and I was able to walk without any discomfort.

We were about half way between the two command centers (a situation that always makes me uneasy because, should the Americans suddenly appear, in which direction would we flee?) on a ridge crest near Chigha Sarai, when I looked up from my musings and saw, sitting on a rocky outcrop not one hundred yards away, a motionless figure. Whoever it was had his back to us and was looking down the valley towards the village of Wama. A fast flowing tributary of the Kunar River tumbled far below him. The man seemed oblivious to our presence.

Abu, who was walking ahead of me, had stopped and was indicating the seated figure by stabbing his Kalashnikov in his direction and looking at me interrogatively. He wanted to shoot the stranger, and was hoping I would give him permission to do so. I knew he would perform this task with as much indifference as he would shoot a rabbit.

We stood on the track for a moment and studied the stranger's back. I looked around us: there was no one else in sight. It was unusual to see people up this high, unless they were Mujahideen or followers of one of the local warlords, and they usually travel in bands. I am kept informed about who is in the area. I know about the comings and goings of everyone, being particularly keen to hear of any strangers who suddenly appear speaking Pashtu or Dari with an American accent. Strangers nearly always mean trouble.

I nodded to Abu, indicating that we should continue on our way. He looked disappointed; he enjoyed target practice. A few yards further on, however, something made me change my mind. I stopped. "We shall go and talk to this stranger."

I turned off the path and headed in the direction of the seated figure, followed by Abu. In fact my bodyguard quickly passed me, obviously having decided he should check out the stranger first to make sure he wasn't an American Special Forces agent.

We reached the spot where the man was sitting. He did not turn round, even though he must surely have heard our approach. The muzzle of Abu's Kalashnikov was inches from the man's back.

"Greetings, stranger," I said. "May Allah be with you."

"Greetings to you, too. To both of you," the man said, without turning round. I wondered how he knew there were two of us. I hadn't seen him so much as glance in our direction.

"May we join you?"

"You are most welcome."

I sat down beside him on the rock, and Abu sat behind us, still holding his rifle at the ready, doubtless praying he would still get the chance to use it. I had not yet seen the man's face, although I could now see the edges of a long, gray beard.

"Allah be praised, it is a very fine day." I have never been good at small talk.

"Indeed it is." We sat side by side in silence for several minutes, staring down into the valley.

After awhile the stranger turned to me, and for the first time I saw his face. There was nothing remarkable about it, from memory, except perhaps his eyes. They were gray and I remember that they shone with a surprising brilliance. He was an old man, possibly in his eighties, but there was a vigor and liveliness about him, a youthful aura, that belied his age. I imagined he would be able to cross the mountains with great speed. And sure enough, when I asked him what he was doing in these parts, he replied that he was a shepherd.

"But where is your flock?" I asked. He waved his hand briefly, indicating that they might be who knows where, it was of little concern to him. He had a quiet but reassuring presence; one did not feel there was much likelihood of anything going wrong while he was around.

Abu, by this time, had lain down behind us, keen to enjoy the sunshine. His rifle lay beside him on the grass, and he was already breathing heavily. So much for my bodyguard.

A little later the old man turned to me and said: "So you are the man they call Osama bin Laden, otherwise known as the Sheikh."

I was pleased to be recognized. My name had even reached this humble shepherd living in the middle of nowhere.

"You have heard of me?" I asked, unable to keep the pride out of my voice.

"Yes, I have heard of you." This was said without much enthusiasm. For the first time in the old man's presence, I felt on my guard.

"And tell me, Osama, are you proud of what you have achieved with your life thus far, those actions that have carried your name to my ears?" His eyes were looking directly into mine, and were open unusually wide, as if he was truly interested in what I might answer. I hesitated for a moment.

"Why yes. Yes, I believe that I am."

"But you are not sure?"

"Yes, I am sure," I said, even though I wasn't. It was he who made me unsure.

Once again we lapsed into silence. Or that is how I remember this. I am writing my diary in the cave, in the evening, as I usually do, and it is not easy to remember exactly the words that were spoken, or the order in which they were said, or when there was a long or a short pause. But I am trying to be as accurate and honest as possible.

Then the old man, the stranger, asked: "You are a great admirer of Sayyid Qutb?"

I nodded my head, wondering where this conversation was heading. I was astonished that an ignorant shepherd should know of Qutb.

"But he was wrong."

I did not answer.

"Qutb was wrong. He made the classic error of allowing an evil, or misguided man, al-Nasser, President of Egypt, to force him into fighting from the wrong corner. His position was not tenable."

"What should he have done in your opinion?" I thought I would humor the stranger and listen to what he had to say.

"Al-Nasser succeeded in driving a wedge between religion and secularism. He wished to show that the two could not co-exist in peace. Qutb accepted that premise when he took up arms against him."

"He had no option."

"He had every option, bin Laden."

I was about to protest, but the old man held up his hand to silence me. I respected his age, and held my tongue.

"The West is evil," he continued. I nodded. "And you Muslim fundamentalists are also evil," he continued.

"We have no—" I started to speak, but he cut me short.

"Listen to me, bin Laden. For the first time, listen to someone. Do not speak."

The old man struck me dumb anyway. No one had spoken to me like that since my nanny, when I was a child.

"The West has many wonderful things going for it. They have their technologies and their industries. They have their computers, their ability to fly into space, their vast cities and communication systems. In the world of materialism, they are both efficient and successful. And they have the ability to change their regimes freely, without bloodshed, without waging war. All of these things can be said to be most admirable.

"Where they go wrong, however, is that they have no soul. Their lives are as empty as the deserts of Arabia and have less meaning than the wanderings of that ant you see before us now. Their spiritual lives are non-existent. That is why they are such an unhappy people. There is no heart in the West, no light."

I could agree with all of that, and so I maintained a respectful silence. Maybe this old man was not as foolish as I had at first thought. I was surprised to find myself sitting on a mountaintop being preached to, because that is what it amounted to, by an old shepherd. But it was an unusual experience, and one that was not so unpleasant in the sunshine, so I remained sitting by his side.

"Us Muslims, we have the spirituality, but we have nothing else. Some are happy to have nothing else but this spirituality, whereas others, the majority, are envious. They look towards the West and they wish they had what they see there. Our task, therefore, is to embrace the things of the West that are admirable, spurn those that are not, yet continue to maintain, nurture and live the way of God."

He lapsed into silence, perhaps giving me an opportunity to digest his words. Behind us, Abu was now snoring. "Your friends down there," and he pointed down the mountainside, "the Taliban, they are not good men. They are misguided also, they do not follow the word of the Qur'an."

I protested. "When they were in power, they ran the Country along strict Muslim lines. Women wore veils—"

"The Qur'an does not oblige women to wear veils, bin Laden."

I ignored that. "They banned television—"

"Is that in the Qur'an?" He smiled at me.

I ignored that remark too. "They introduced stonings and mutilations—an eye for an eye, and a tooth for a tooth."

"Those are not literal. The Qur'an was talking metaphorically."

"I do not believe so. I think it was meant literally," I replied, but could not think of any argument to support my hypothesis.

"The Taliban used our great religion as a tool of oppression. They are in the main Pakhtuns, and they treated every other ethnic group with disdain. Where does it praise such practices in the Qur'an? Rather, it teaches that Muslims must not fight against other Muslims, that they must live in harmony together.

"The Qur'an I know, study and love says that all religions must be respected, that Islam is no more and no less of the answer than Judaism, Christianity, Buddhism or Hinduism. It says that the great prophets like Abraham, Moses, David, Solomon and Jesus have as much right to preach to their followers as the Prophet Muhammad. The Prophet's message was no different to their message. He himself preached tolerance. He condemned, in the plainest of language, all wars of aggression."

I was unable to restrain myself any more. "We do not love aggression either, but we are driven to it by the evil of the West. Muslims have been attacked, and are under attack, by the West and we are forced to respond. The Qur'an states that this is permissible. To fight in self-defense is permissible."

"Islam is a religion of peace. And in all circumstances it condemns the slaughter of innocent civilians."

I quoted the Sword Verse from the Qur'an: "'And when the sacred months are over, kill the polytheists wherever you find them, and take them captive, and besiege them, and lie in wait for them in every stratagem of war.' It is the will of God, old man."

"You cannot wash your hands of your own responsibility for your actions, bin Laden. It is a time for toleration. We will only reach the end of this millennia if we can show tolerance towards each other."

"How can we be expected to be tolerant when the Americans are in Saudi Arabia, trampling over our holy sites? How can we be tolerant when they invade Iraq and steal our oil? How can we be tolerant when they support, with weapons and money, the Israelis in their battle to push Palestinians from their homeland, when they attempt to wipe Palestine off the face of the earth? How can we be tolerant in the face of all of that? Answer me that, o keeper of the sheep, answer me that."

He studied my face in silence. I was angry with myself for getting angry, while he remained so calm.

"With goodwill, all is possible. In Turkey, Morocco and Indonesia the people maintain their religious beliefs while embracing some of the ways of the West."

"Those countries are jahiliyyah(12)."

"Is that why you bomb them?"

I nodded. He turned down the corners of his mouth to show he did not comprehend this. "They are taking a way that may not be your way, but it does not mean that it is the wrong way. It is simply a different way. They are Muslim countries, is that not enough for you?"

"No, it is not enough. The Americans are intent on taking over such countries—they are intent on taking over the world and wiping Muslims off the face of the earth."

"Is that so? Then why are there Muslims in America, bin Laden? Tell me that. They perform salat and live good and holy lives without any trouble. They are left in peace by their fellow citizens."

"They are tolerated, nothing more. Their time will come."

"If that is so, maybe it is because of you. It is maybe you who causes trouble for our brothers in America, could that not be so?"

"I am fighting to win freedom for Muslims everywhere, to wipe out tyranny."

"Only the ulema(13) can declare a jihad."

"There is no ulema in our time, you know that."

"So you think that gives you the authority?" There was scorn in his voice for the first time. "If you would learn to be more accepting of other people and of other religions, bin Laden, then perhaps everyone could live in peace.

"It says in the Qur'an that the slaying of one innocent person is tantamount to the slaying of all humanity. So how can you involve yourself in the slaying of innocent individuals, of innocent human beings? The logic of history has proven many times that violence is not the way to achieve a desired end. Those who resort to violence are those who lack logic."

I stood up, angry. "Why don't you tell that to the Americans, old man?" I kicked Abu awake. He opened his eyes, reaching for his rifle. "We're going."

The old man smiled up at me, shielding his eyes against the sun. "I would tell them exactly that if they were to come and ask me."

Abu looked at me quizzically. "You want me to waste him, boss?"

I wish he wouldn't always speak in the language of the Mafia. I shook my head.

"No. We're leaving."

Without another word to the old man I strode off, followed by Abu. The old man called after us: "May Allah, the most Merciful and the most Compassionate, accompany you on your journey."

I walked the rest of the way in silence. The old man had upset me. He was a fool. I did not believe his arguments, and I had heard most of them before, but he had still upset me. He obviously did not appreciate the extent of the Americans' evil.

When we arrived at the next command center, Abu said off-handedly to the others: "Did you guys see that old freak on the way here?"

No one had. No one had seen anyone.

October 24.

My deputy in Iraq, Abu Musab al-Zarqawi, is carrying on a fine fight against the enemy. He looks so like a middle-aged bank clerk, or even a nondescript Pentagon official that I sometimes have a problem taking him seriously, but he is doing an excellent job, and keeping the name of al-Qaeda up there in lights.

October 30.

Did not take one Valium yesterday. How good is that!

Keen to put Ayman in his place, I released my own video. It was my idea that I be filmed behind a desk looking very political. I wore a traditional robe in glorious gold, and a white headdress. Ayman was, of course, quick to criticize. He made a typically catty remark about how I looked like a self-made American millionaire, the kind you see hanging out in Florida all the time. "Where are your gold chains, Osama?" he asked. He's just jealous. I thought I looked great—and so did Abu. Gold really suits me.

I gave the Americans a bit of a different spiel this time: less of the jihad, and more of a political statement. I thought I came across as quite statesmanlike.

Hopefully, releasing the video just before the election, and reminding voters that I'm still at large, will swing it Bush's way. I also cut back on the violence and mayhem angle a bit. Voters are after reassurance; they don't like change. Ayman's worried that it may give votes to Kerry, but what does he know. He hasn't got a strategic brain in his head.

November 3.

Have been up all night watching the election results.

It looks as if my tactics have been successful: Bush has won. I opened some champagne and toasted him. I wonder if he'll write and thank me for my help. I sent him a short email, anyway, simply saying, "Go, Georgie, go!"

Of course, he has probably already thanked Karl Rove. It was his bright idea to come up with some excuses for an invasion of Iraq—even though Saddam had absolutely nothing to do with 9/11—because Mr. Potato Head realized that an incumbent President fighting a war is almost certain to be re-elected. And he was right.

Laura looked delectable on the podium—although I was upset when she put her arms around the retard Texan. She appears quite diminutive at his side, and I never cease to wonder what she sees in him. He really does look as if he has just stepped off the ranch. *Aw, gee, shucks, you guys!* he mutters in his high-pitched voice, spitting 'baccy across the room, splashing the shoes of his missus, while he hitches up his pants, scratches his privates, and belches. He makes LBJ seem positively sophisticated. And I swear his eyes have grown even closer together since he won. Soon he'll look like a Martian, with just one eye in the center of his forehead

The most upsetting thing about the man, however, is the way he regards the Presidency as his right. I suppose this comes from his background. It's like he actually believes he was born to be President—even though he's supposedly the stupidest man who has ever sat in the Oval Office. He is so arrogant. Certainly he does not know the meaning of the word humility.

November 5.

Some Lebanese journo has reacted to my latest video by calling me "a multi-dimensional psychopath." Not sure what this means, even though it sounds quite flattering, but I suspect that it is not a compliment. I shall take it as one nevertheless.

November 11.

Have written to Pat Robertson, the televangelist and right wing political activist, and asked if Karl Himmler Rove has yet, as promised, "fucked him like he has never been fucked before." I'm fascinated to know. It may open up some new techniques and positions that I am as yet unaware of.

November 14.

Colin Powell has resigned as Secretary of State, and been replaced by Condoleezza Rice. One token black replaced by another. Not only is she better looking, but she'll go along with everything the Boss suggests. A rubber stamp pure and simple.

November 15.

The Americans are crawling all over the place. Why don't they go home and leave me in peace? It's too cold to be out and about in weather like this. I'd rather be lying by a pool somewhere in the sunshine.

This afternoon I had a moment alone with Samah. I said to her that she owed it to me, as her boss, to take care of my needs, but she said her duty was to remain faithful to Mohammed. I wish I had taken more care to please her that first time we were together; she might be more considerate to me now.

December 9.

Barbara Walters has named Karl Rove the "Most Fascinating Person" of the year. I mean, *really,* how short-sighted is that! Who is she trying to kid? Has she met no one else all year? I think she has finally lost her marbles. What about Paris Hilton, Tom Hanks, Mickey Rourke, Michael Douglas, Charlton Heston…? Think of the riveting conversations one could have with any of them. There are so many other, better qualified people than Mr. Potato Head.

December 10.

Laura seems to be changing her image. Gone are the frowsy, blowsy, buttoned-up-to-the-neck clothes of yesterday. Now it's Oscar De La Renta and Caroline Herrarra. Who's she getting all dressed up for, that's what I want to know? Could she be trying to send me some kind of message? It's possible, although she may simply be making a last ditch effort to stop Bushy falling asleep at nine o'clock.

Maybe I should buy Samah some designer underwear? Might get me some action, but I'm not sure how it would go down with Mohammed.

December 20.

Georgie Porgie has been voted TIME magazine's "Man of the Year." Wonder how much he had to pay for that "honor." Would write and congratulate him, except that it has become a meaningless honor ever since they passed me over. Imagine that the White House dictated the choice anyway. They control the Press—in that the fourth estate is too damned scared to publish anything he would disapprove of.

December 23.

Great uproar around the world. Armed robbers have stolen £22 million from the Northern Bank in Ireland. Everyone's pointing the finger at the IRA, which makes me laugh. They're well and truly fooled. The IRA certainly carried out the robbery, but it was on my behalf, and they're only receiving ten per cent for their trouble. Mind you, that publicity-seeking maniac, Gerry Adams, will be only too happy to take all the credit. It should give him a few more hours in front of the cameras. I did all the planning, however—the hard bit—so I deserve the majority of the spoils.

Anyway, the IRA is a spent force, its leaders continually talking about decommissioning their weapons, which I have offered to buy, and making peace with their enemy. One simply cannot trust Christians, any Christians, whether Protestant or Catholic. Quite untrustworthy, the lot of them. The IRA is now talking about gaining power through the ballot box. How pathetic is that! They'll be sitting in parliament next, and talking.

Suffering great irritation from my piles, and I've run out of cream. Ayman, laughing loudly, offered to operate. That man really is perverse.

December 29.

Another year almost past, and as usual it seems to have flown by. I find the end of the year—any year—depressing. I look back and wonder what I have achieved. More than almost any man on earth is the answer, of course, but I am still dissatisfied. So imagine how ordinary mortals must feel!

I am tired being continually on the run, hiding in caves, doing without many of the basics of life. I would never admit as much to any of my followers, but that, in all honesty, is how I feel. Maybe next year will bring improved fortunes.

I need a Valium and to turn in.

Night-night, Os.

Some words found in this Diary

1. *Hijab*. The veil worn by many Muslim women.

2. *Kufiyya* and *agal*. Traditional Arab head cloth held in place by heavy woolen coils (*agal*.)

3. *Hajj*. Annual pilgrimage to Mecca that every Muslim must undertake once in his lifetime.

4. *Alim*. A learned man, and guardian of the legal and religious traditions of Islam.

5. *Salat*. The prayers Muslims make five times daily.

6. *Zakat*, A fixed proportion of every Muslim's income that must go towards helping the poor.

7. *Sajjada*. Prayer mat.

8. *Loar sheik*. Big chief.

9. Holy Tuesday. The term often used by al-Qaeda to refer to 9/11.

10. *al-'abda*. The slave. Nickname earned because bin Laden's mother, Hamida, was Syrian.

11. ISI. Pakistan's intelligence service.

12. *Jahiliyyah*. A society that has turned its back on God.

13. *Ulema*. Community of scholars and theologians.

978-0-595-38095-4
0-595-38095-6

Printed in the United States
50088LVS00003B/105